SELECTIVE MEMORY

Jennifer L. Jordan

Spinsters Ink
2007

Spinsters Ink
P.O. Box 242
Midway, Florida 32343

Printed in the United States of America on acid-free paper
First Edition

Editor: Christi Cassidy
Cover designer: LA Callaghan

ISBN-10: 1-883523-88-5
ISBN-13: 978-1-883523-88-6

For those who can't forget . . .

About the Author

Jennifer L. Jordan, a Lambda Literary Award Finalist, is the author of *A Safe Place To Sleep, Existing Solutions, Commitment To Die, Unbearable Losses* and *Disorderly Attachments*, all mysteries in the Kristin Ashe series. For more information or to read excerpts of her books, visit her Web site at www.JenniferLJordan.com.

Kristin Ashe Mysteries by Jennifer L. Jordan

Selective Memory

Disorderly Attachments

Unbearable Losses

Commitment To Die

Existing Solutions

A Safe Place To Sleep

PROLOGUE

They think I can't remember, but I can.

Every weekday afternoon, I vow never to come again.

I sense I have reached a point beyond all reason, but I can't stop.

Watching her.

Wanting her.

In the waning light of winter, I stay for hours, often until long past the moment of darkness.

I feel helpless to do anything but stare, stare at her silhouette.

These are the last images I remember before millions of my brain cells died.

CHAPTER 1

"They think I'm crazy, but I'm not."

"Who thinks you're crazy?" I said neutrally.

"Stacey and my mother."

I smiled. "What do partners and family know?"

Alexandra Madigen frowned. "I don't trust Stacey's impressions."

"Were the two of you close before the accident?"

"After eleven years, we must have been, but why does she feel so far away?"

"Do you remember anything about your life before the accident?"

"Fragments, but I can't tell if the random memories belong to me or someone else. I hear dissonant sounds. Crickets chirping. Sheets of rain falling. Weeping. Bells ringing. A bathroom stall door slamming. But I've lost all sense of time and place and belonging."

"It takes time—"

"That's what I've been told, but I don't have time. Stacey hugs me, and I recoil. A relief nurse comes in, and I feel at ease. My mother recounts stories from the past, and I disconnect. Strangers stop by, and I connect. I need to trust someone." She pointed at me, almost stabbing me in the forehead with her finger. "I choose you."

"Why me?"

"Because you don't know me. You never have."

"You're not afraid of what I'll find?"

Her eyes narrowed. "I nearly died nine months ago."

"Meaning nothing scares you anymore?"

"Meaning, I'm more terrified of not knowing."

I took a deep breath. "Fair enough."

"Next month I'll be released from Sinclair and sent to live with Stacey. I need to prepare myself." Alex studied me. "Do you think I'm crazy?"

I tried not to flinch under her gaze. "Ask me again in a few weeks."

"Are you always this honest?"

"No," I said truthfully.

I would have employed more tact, but something about Alex Madigen had stripped away my pretenses. In our first minutes together, she'd shown me the marks on her body from her high-speed car crash and nine operations, a matter-of-fact demonstration devoid of self-pity. She pointed out the shallow depression in the back of her head from drilling to relieve pressure on her brain, the line in her throat from placement of a ventilator, the tracks on her stomach from emergency surgery to save her liver and the scars on her back from the insertion of titanium rods and pins. Her invisible inventory included a broken femur, cracked ribs and bruised kidneys.

Remarkably, her oval face and flawless complexion had been untouched by the impact. Her small mouth housed an arrangement of perfect teeth, and her brilliant blue eyes conveyed a stunning clarity.

I shifted my weight on the folding chair, causing a loud squeak amplified by the linoleum. "Kelly tells me you owned your own advertising agency. Do you remember any of that?"

"Odd jingles run through my head." Alex ran a hand through her blondish-brown hair, which was cut in a textured style that barely covered her ears. She sang under her breath, "Don't groan if you can't get a loan. All you need is a name that's good, come on down to Henny's 'hood."

I laughed. "I've seen that one on TV. A commercial for Henny Carmichael's dealership. Did you enjoy your work?"

"I don't know. Did it pay well? Does Stacey want my money?"

I hesitated. "I don't know why she would."

"How old am I?"

"Thirty-seven."

"How old are you?"

"The same age."

She nodded thoughtfully. "Need to get around town, but no money down? Never fear, no payments till next year. Do I love Stacey?"

"You must have, or you wouldn't have stayed together."

"What unusual logic."

"Thanks," I said, opting to interpret the remark as a compliment.

"Are you in a relationship?"

"Yes."

"And?"

"With Destiny Greaves. She's an activist who runs the Lesbian Community Center. We've been together four years."

"Did you follow her before you met?"

"Her career? Somewhat. Destiny's hard to miss. She's in the news all the time."

"Do you still love her?"

"Of course."

For the hundredth time, Alex waved to a resident twenty feet away who was stringing red, white and blue beads on safety pins. "Do you love her as much?"

"As what?"

"As before?"

"Yes."

"Has she hurt you?"

I squirmed. "At times."

"Irreparably?"

"I hope not."

"Have you harmed her?"

"Not on purpose."

"If you've loved, you've damaged," Alex said without inflection.

I cleared my throat. "We're getting a little off track. Were you always like this?"

"Like what?"

"Adept at deflecting attention away from yourself?"

She released a cynical smile. "Yes, I believe I was. Do I have friends?"

"I'm sure you do."

"Why haven't they come to see me?"

"Kelly told me Stacey and your mom thought you'd do better with less stimulation."

They think I can't remember, but I can.

Stacey was a counselor.

She took care of people in their hour of torture, a calling that had exacted a toll on her. Sometimes, I wondered what she would have been like if she'd become a midwife, participating in the beginnings, not the endings.

Every year we stayed together, she closed another part of herself to me. I tried to reopen them but soon moved on to lamenting the lost pieces of her. One day, without realizing it, I stopped missing what was missing. The person I'd met, fallen in love with and committed to had left, but I settled for the one who remained.

Her clients and colleagues received the best of her, and who was I to fight with death? What just reason gave me the right to demand the same caring and compassion she showered on others when I wasn't in crisis? I never sent Stacey letters of appreciation or bestowed a service medal on her. I simply believed that our time together should have been reward enough.

Until one day, I stopped believing that.

· · ·

After a ten-second silence, Alex said, "Why have I been forbidden stimulation?"

"You're recovering from major injuries, including a closed-head trauma."

"My brain was hurt?"

"Yes, and the injury causes you to become easily confused or agitated."

She cocked her head. "Do I seem confused or agitated?"

"Not now, no."

"I used to stare into space for hours."

"Immediately after the accident?"

"Immediately before. Did you know I had a dog? Cooper. I met him this weekend, on my home visit with Stacey. He seems to like me."

I smiled. "Dogs are great judges of character."

"I want to see my friends."

"Okay," I said easily. "I'll clear it with Stacey."

Alex stared at me. "Does her name have to be on our contract?"

"No. The agreement I draw up can be between you and me. An hourly rate, plus expenses."

"Nothing gets cleared with Stacey. Is that clear?"

I showed no emotion. "Clear."

"Who are you again?"

"I'm Kristin Ashe. I'm a private investigator. Kelly Nagle introduced us an hour ago, and you decided to hire me."

"Who's Kelly Nagle? Is she qualified to make a referral?"

"She should be. She's your case manager, and her specialty is neurological injuries."

"I see." She extended her hand, and we shook again. "Why am I hiring you?"

"To help you recover your memories," I said, suppressing a sigh.

This wasn't going as well as I'd hoped.

When Kelly Nagle had called the day before, I'd expressed skepticism about helping a brain-injured woman. "Just meet her," Kelly had implored, and I'd acceded, an agreement I regretted shortly after stepping into the activities room at Sinclair Rehabilitation Center, a facility located on the northern edge of Denver.

Alex Madigen had been playing classical music on a battered upright piano. Dressed in a tuxedo shirt, pearls, jeans and no shoes, she seemed unaware of the residents and staff around her. As they engaged in computer training, quiet conversation and games, Alex played on flawlessly, as if she'd been hired to provide background music.

This won't be too bad, I thought, and then the music had stopped.

When Kelly stepped forward to compliment Alex on her playing, Alex wouldn't acknowledge her. Instead, she pounded the keys and broke into a harsh, sarcastic rendition of a jingle. "Turn your crash into cash. You have the right to sue. Yes, you do. Yes, you do. Call our office today. We'll make someone pay."

After finishing the jingle, she stood and stretched, tilted her head toward the sunlight streaming in through the windows behind her and rested her hands at her sides. Eventually, with Kelly's gentle persuasion, Alex reclaimed her seat at the piano bench and accepted that I'd come to see her, not someone else at Sinclair.

Since Kelly had left us alone, Alex had hired me, fired me and forgotten me three times.

Alex suddenly closed the piano with a bang. "What did Kelly Nagle tell you about me?"

"Only that you've made an amazing recovery."

"So they say, but no one can predict how I'll turn out. Least of all me. When will I remember everything?"

"Everything? No one does, with or without a brain injury. Is it important that you do?"

She pumped the piano pedals, as if testing their tension for the first time. "It's essential."

"Why do you think you need memories?"

"To remind me of who I am. Without them, I'm forced to rely on other people's impressions."

"Or you can be whoever you want to be, completely free of

expectations—your own or anyone else's."

She shook her head. "I refuse to make the same mistakes. I need my memories back. All of them."

"Even with visits from friends and information from the interviews I'll conduct, that won't necessarily happen," I said cautiously.

One by one, Alex placed sheets of music into a large, plastic folder, her movements stiff and awkward. "Kelly says that's the hardest loss I'll face, loss of identity. But I refuse to let go."

"You might not have a choice, if—"

Her voice rose. "If I don't get my memories back, how will I know who I am?"

"Was," I said quietly.

"Am. Can I hold on to the illusion that I lived my life completely and honorably?"

"Tell me what you remember."

Alex pressed the folder of music to her chest. "Some memories I clutch until I've strangled them. Others I dodge in order to evade injury."

"Injury?"

"I remain still for hours, and nothing appears. Other times, I'm in the middle of an activity and something interrupts."

"You're probably more sensitive to the randomness, but that's how memory works. A sound, smell, phrase—anything can trigger it. This morning at Starbucks, I smelled a perfume that reminded me of my first girlfriend."

Alex broke from watching a patient wheel into the room and turned idly to look at me. "Did you lose yourself in her?"

I started. "My first girlfriend? Yes, I did."

She tried to disguise a wince of pain. "I believe I did, too."

They think I can't remember, but I can.

I sat in my car, staring at a three-story, brick building, waiting for the woman who lived in the southeast corner of the second floor to arrive.

This wasn't my first vigil, nor my last.

At five o'clock, a late-model Volvo pulled up and parked five car lengths ahead of my Toyota.

When the dark-haired woman stepped out of her car, my pulse quickened, and I lowered myself in the seat, fearful of a glance that never came.

On this day, not unlike many others, the woman never looked around. She reached into the backseat, retrieved a purse and walked briskly into the building. From a box that hung in the tiny space between two glass doors, she gathered her mail, correspondence I'd already scanned.

Moments later, she entered her apartment, turned on a light in the front room and, behind sheer curtains, moved gracefully.

If only she would have turned so that I could see her face.

"Alex!"

Alex opened her eyes wide. "What?"

"Are you sure you want to do this?"

"Am I sure . . ." Her voice faded, and she closed her eyes again.

"Did a memory come back to you just then? Was it about your first girlfriend?"

"I must have drifted off."

As the noise in the activities room intensified, I leaned forward to hear her. "Does that happen often?"

She slid back reflexively, almost tumbling off the bench. "Apparently. I dream frequently, but I don't know whether the images come from my life or someone else's."

"Can you talk about them?"

She blinked rapidly. "The time isn't right for articulation."

"Maybe you could keep a journal. Write down everything as it comes to you."

"A chronicle of the life I've lost. I'll consider that," she said before transferring her attention to a handwritten note on the piano. *Take music back to room.* She seized the bright green piece of paper and tucked it below her leg.

"I use notes myself sometimes," I said.

She avoided my gaze. "The reminders sustained me in the beginning, but I'm striving to decrease my dependency. I suppose it's a victory that I no longer have to tell myself to chew before swallowing."

"It probably helps to focus on the gains."

"On moving forward, always forward. Three weeks in intensive care. Another month in the hospital. Seven months at Sinclair. Next month out."

"Nine months of working on your body—that can't be easy."

"It seems like longer, as if my other life never existed."

"Kelly tells me you're one of the most motivated people she's met, that you have an intense desire to get healthy."

Alex shrugged indifferently. "I need my independence back."

"Do you feel ready to go home?"

She shivered violently. "Home? I can't go there."

"Why?"

"I lost it. Shortly before the accident. I'd been . . . with a . . ."

I waited, but when she didn't finish the sentence, I prompted, "A friend? A relative?"

Her face turned ashen. "With her."

CHAPTER 2

"One hundred and eighty-four days until opening day," Fran Green said to me happily a few hours later, opening remarks for my arrival back at the office.

I tossed my keys and notepad onto the desk. "The ski area only closed last month."

"Wish it would snow."

"It's May fourteenth."

"It could happen."

I gave her a pained smile. "Don't start."

She offered me a gumball from her desktop machine, but I declined. The last one I'd accepted tasted like a cross between peppermint and incense and almost extracted one of my crowns. I brushed pieces of confetti from my desk to hers and borrowed one of her *Charlie's Angels* coasters for my Big Gulp. Fran had tricked out her work area with toys, gadgets, stuffed animals and party favors, while I'd decorated with a blotter, lamp, organizing basket and photo of Destiny. We'd splurged recently and purchased matching high-back leather chairs that tilted and swiveled, and at the moment, Fran was testing hers to the limits, her feet propped on the windowsill.

Our agency address was on Sixth Avenue, just north of Cherry Creek, a trendy area in Denver known for its tree-lined streets, specialty boutiques, five-star restaurants and million-dollar townhomes. We were close enough to enjoy the ambiance, yet far enough away to afford the rent. Tucked between a flower shop and a secondhand clothing store, our ground-floor office, at eight hundred square feet, was divided into three rooms, with a narrow hallway that ran from front to back. Most of the time, Fran and I sat practically on top of each other in the front room, at adjoining desks where we enjoyed natural light and an unobstructed view of passersby.

Fran flipped the pages on her wall calendar. "I'll need November fourteenth off for snowboarding. First day of the new season. That'd be a Wednesday. Could make up the hours the following Saturday. Unless there's fresh powder," she said, jutting out her chest. Fran was known for her eclectic collection of message shirts, and today's read, *Four Inches of Powder Equals One Sick Day.*

I sighed. "How did your appointment go?"

She beamed. "You're hired."

"Me?" My voice fractured. "This was your idea."

"Can't be helped. Client chose you."

"How?"

"From our portfolio."

"Portfolio! Who's in it?"

"You. Me."

"That's it? Tell me this is a joke."

"No joke. You have an appointment with Roxanne Herbert on Thursday, at high noon."

"No, no, no! What were you thinking?"

"Better sit down and breathe. Let me give you the details." Fran waited for me to fall into my chair. "Used that picture I took of you and Destiny on the raft trip. Cropped out your honey, of course. Decent shot of you. Shows off your busty build and cute legs. Probably why Roxie chose you. Got me beat on height and hair, too.

Target's more in your age range. Can't feel bad about myself. Next one'll come my way. Can't wait. Easiest money we'll make."

Fran Green, an ex-nun, was sixty-seven years old, barely cleared five feet, sported a gray crew cut and had a flat chest. At the age of thirty-seven, I, an ex-Catholic, had no more than a dozen gray hairs sprinkled among medium-length brown ones, listed my height as five-six on my driver's license, only a slight exaggeration, and had breasts large enough to quash any attempt at a professional sports career.

Unless something changed drastically, I'd be shouldering the load on every decoy job.

I shook my head and groaned. "Why did I let you talk me in to this?"

"Maybe 'cause you know we need another stream of income. Diversity, that's the key to success in any private eye organization. Infidelity's always in season, and decoy cases, that's where the money's at."

I rolled my eyes.

I'd met Fran four years earlier, and what had begun as a professional acquaintance had quickly grown into friendship, eventually evolving into a loose business arrangement. At the beginning of the year, we'd formalized our partnership by forming a limited liability corporation with a fifty-fifty split, a percentage I often rued.

"Consider it a public service," she continued merrily. "Say a wife suspects the other half of cheating but has limited resources. Full-fee surveillance adds up pretty quickly at a Ben Franklin per hour. Decoy service gives 'em a cost-effective alternative. Wife chooses a decoy from our portfolio of women's photographs, the one most likely to tempt her beloved."

"You told me you were going to find independent contractors, that I wouldn't have to be involved directly. That—"

"Haven't had time. Went to test the waters, and the first response came sooner than expected."

I rubbed my forehead. "What do I have to do?"

"Easy steps. Interview the wife and devise a strategy to bump into the target. Tape-record all contacts with the target and turn them over to said wife. She'll decide how far, if at all, spouse has strayed. Slick, quick deal. Three hundred smackers per meeting. Wife preapproves every encounter. Any questions?"

Three hundred dollars. The price of my soul. "Tell me again why this isn't unethical."

Fran waved a hand dismissively. "Some firms won't go after the business 'cause they consider it entrapment. But guess who owns those agencies? Men who cheat. From a feminist perspective, we're providing a valuable service. Tell me how many women can divert larges sums to hire a detective without attracting the notice of their mate. We'll follow accepted industry practices. The decoy—"

"Meaning me."

"Meaning you. You'll meet the target in public. Only allowed to initiate eye contact. Nothing more. If you meet through business or recreation, only permitted to introduce yourself. All professional, everything on the up and up. If a spouse tries to cheat with a decoy, no question vows'd be broken under other circumstances. Decoying cuts to the chase. I like it," she said, nodding her approval.

"How did you find the client?"

"Roxanne answered my Test-A-Mate ad in *Westword*. Catchy title, ain't it? Hope you don't mind. Named the division without consulting you, but open to feedback before I place the next ad."

"The name's fine." I bit my lip. "What do I have to do?"

"Quick refresher. Where's that notebook they gave me at the seminar?" Fran put her feet on the floor and rotated until she faced the bookshelf behind her. She grabbed a red binder with a broken heart graphic on the cover and glanced at a page in the middle. "No outward moves on your part. Light flirting and following the target's lead are permissible, but no sex. No matter what. One touch could expose us to a lawsuit. *Bam*, the agency's gone."

"No touching, no problem," I said tersely.

"Shouldn't be with you. Gotta warn you. Might have to endure an attempted pass—hand-holding, a peck, some groping—but cut it off immediately. Got it?"

I felt faint. "Yes."

Fran handed me a cell phone. "Give this number to the target and carry the phone with you twenty-four-seven. Needs to be turned on at all times. Take it to bed with you. Targets like to call early in the morning and late at night."

I eyed the phone as if it were varnished with germs. "Where did you get this?"

"Disposable. Don't want anything tying back to us."

"I've got this other case, Alex Madigen. The memory loss. How am I supposed to do both?"

"No problem there. I'll pitch in with the amnesia. Give me a task, and it'll get done."

"How much time will this decoy thing take?"

"Can't say. Have to buckle down and burn the midnight oil, need be. Might be one meeting or ten. Leave that up to the client. Play our cards right, this could develop into a cash cow. Put a couple of bombshells in the portfolio, no telling how far we can go."

"Let's just complete one case successfully."

"My thinking exactly. Improve our odds if you could spruce up your attire. Anything sexy or slinky in your closet? See-through shirts, short skirts? Fishnets, three-inch spikes?"

"Only slight upgrades from this," I said tightly, indicating my short-sleeve, white mock turtleneck, blue jeans and black loafers.

She made a sucking noise. "Any pants that show the crack? You could pull it off." I glared at her, and she handed me a tape recorder the size of a credit card. "Moving on, here's the new Olympus. Silent auto stop. Capable of three hours of recording."

"Three hours!"

Fran squinted and nodded. "Might need every inch of tape. Decoy assignations can drag on. Tape-record all the meetings and make a dupe. One for our records, one for the client."

"This is making me sick to my stomach."

"Toughen up, kiddo. We're messengers, not instigators. Thicken the skin and stay detached." Fran scratched her chin. "Not always about sex, you know. Strangest things on these tapes infuriate wives. Read about one target who claimed his wife died from a brain aneurysm, when she'd actually survived. Common for the scoundrels to deny they have kids, eliminating the wee ones soon as they pull out of the driveway. Ugly business, but lucrative."

I opened my top desk drawer. "Okay. Give me the information for the appointment. I'll write it on my calendar."

"There's one catch," Fran said with a sneaky smile.

I slammed the drawer and eyed her steadily. "What?"

"The target's a woman. Linda Palizzi."

My head slumped to my chest. "You want me to trap a lesbian cheating on a lesbian?"

"Shame on you. We tempt, never trap."

Luring a lesbian. How was I going to explain this to Destiny? Carefully, I thought, right after I explained it to myself. Fortunately or unfortunately, I had twenty-two days to ponder the phrasing. Currently, my partner was attending a conference in San Francisco, an extended brainstorming session with other lesbian activists from across the country. Their mission was to come away from the symposium with a uniform approach to gay marriage and domestic partnerships. With a dose of guile, I could hide this decoy mess from Destiny on our daily phone calls and package it in a tidy, redacted summary by the time she returned.

"Whatever," I croaked. "A lesbian? I have to go after a lesbian?"

"Yes, indeed. Why's that different?"

I took off my glasses, covered my eyes and let out a moan. "It just is."

CHAPTER 3

"I don't know why you're doing this," Stacey Wilhite said to me crossly the next day at noon.

Alex Madigen's partner and I were seated on a bench in the middle of Washington Park, enjoying a front-row view of a road that served as a training course for runners, inline skaters and cyclists.

"It's a pointless exercise," she continued as the greyhound lying by her feet yawned. "Gathering up people for visits and interviewing them about Alex's past and personality. If you want to do something useful, teach Alex occupational skills or work with her on physical therapy movements. Babysit her for an afternoon or take her home for the weekend."

"I'm doing this," I replied with composure, "because Alex threatened you with a lawsuit to revoke the medical proxy if you wouldn't allow me access. She wants contact with someone other than you and her mother. Someone from the outside world. Her world."

"Alex's caseworkers told me to minimize stimulation," Stacey said defensively. "Physical contact, phone calls and visits were supposed to be limited."

"It's been nine months."

"No one's exactly lining up for the privilege."

I bristled. "What do you mean by that?"

"Alex has no friends."

"Since the accident?"

"Or before. Except for Cooper." She gestured unkindly at the dog, who lay on his side, eyes half-open. "And he has no personality. Alex wanted to rescue a greyhound because she said they don't ask to be born into a life of kenneling and racing or deserve to be discarded when they stop performing. She'd heard greyhounds were docile, but this one's ridiculous. I hate coming to the park, and I hate walking him, which Alex used to do. She was a loner, even before . . ." Stacey paused, seeming to edit herself. "Before she drove into a concrete barrier."

"Yesterday as I was leaving, Alex asked about Derek. Who is he?"

Stacey laughed, a cruel noise that brought attention to her thin lips and slight overbite. She had sunken cheeks and eyes and dark irises that hinted at long-standing disillusionment. Her hair, short and dark, was brittle from product. "She's asking for Derek Wallace? Isn't that hilarious?"

"Who is he?" I repeated.

"A boy who used to live down the street from us." She moved her foot abruptly after the dog tried to lay his head on it. She must not have wanted dog hairs to sully her blue toe-loop sandals or, God forbid, creep up and cling to her cerulean pantsuit or periwinkle embroidered shell.

"Could I get in touch with Derek?"

"Alex hasn't told you?"

"Told me what?"

Stacey laughed again, not bothering to explain the inside joke. "I'll give you his mother's phone number. Dianna will explain everything."

"Thank you," I said, trying to remain civil. "Also, Alex showed me her room, and I noticed a photo of her with a chorus. Did she have friends in that organization? Could any of them come visit?"

Stacey scoffed. "Her mom brought in that picture to remind Alex of her musical career, such as it was in recent years. A few chorus members stopped by when Alex was in the hospital, but I asked them to leave. Nothing was the same after Alex joined their group."

"Which was when?"

"I don't know," she said irritably. "Eighteen months ago."

"Did you have couples friends or acquaintances, someone she might remember?"

"Between my work and Alex's inertia, we didn't have a wide circle. Or any circle, for that matter."

"What type of work do you do? Alex couldn't remember."

"I'm a grief counselor, employed by the Denver Coroner's Office in the victims' assistance unit. I make the kind of house calls you never want to get."

"How are you holding up, dealing with Alex's accident?"

"I'm managing."

"It must be difficult."

Stacey stared straight ahead, toward the lake, where a flock of geese skimmed across the water before taking off in flight. "I took a three-month leave of absence to be with Alex. Ever since I returned to work, I've felt myself going through the motions. I can't set aside my concerns to help people with every little thing they need," she said wearily. "It takes years to recover physically, emotionally and financially from unexpected loss, but the first hours and days are the hardest. I used to be able to reach out to people and assure them they'd survive."

"Not anymore?"

She shrugged. "Not as well as before."

"How did you hear about Alex's accident?"

"Someone from the hospital called. He'd found my number in Alex's phone." Stacey stopped abruptly. "I thought I understood the devastation that comes with the sudden and arbitrary. Screaming, crying, falling to the ground. I've seen it all."

"How did you react?"

She looked me square in the eye. "I laughed at the irony."

"What was ironic about—"

"Alex has the audacity to threaten to sue me to relinquish my role as caregiver. Isn't that rich?" She clasped her hands together. "Over the weekend, I brought her home for a trial run. Did she tell you about our two days together?"

"No. How did they go?"

"Extremely well, unless you include the part about her being nervous and begging me not to leave. She became clammy and nauseated if I wasn't next to her every minute. I have a habit of pacing when I talk on the phone, and she followed me around for an hour while I spoke with my sister, with the dog tramping after her. The three of us, in a train, doing laps around the condo."

"I didn't know—"

"She had night tremors, and I had to leave the door ajar every time I went to the bathroom. I took a nap, and she left the water running in the tub and flooded the bathroom. She kept losing a crystal one of the nurses had given her and shrieking. She apologized repeatedly, but the desperation never left her eyes." Stacey leaned forward aggressively. "Do you really believe Alex can't remember?"

"I have no reason not to believe her. Do you?"

"Her amnesia comes and goes, which I consider a form of manipulation. She's able to pretend her life didn't exist before August sixteenth."

"The date of her accident?"

Stacey smiled cynically. "The date of impact. Life before that, well, it appears she'll conveniently allow in the parts she likes and erase others."

"Don't we all filter, to some extent?"

"Obviously, she has you under a spell."

I looked at her carefully. "Do you hate her?"

"I lived in Saint Luke's hospital with Alex for weeks. I was there when no one could tell me whether she'd live or die. After she came out of the coma, I visited her two or three times a day, for hours at a time. I've been her medical advocate, calling for conferences with doctors, nurses and therapists, forcing specialists to talk to one another, fighting with insurance companies and medical billing departments, checking hundreds, and I mean hundreds, of medical bills. I've brought in her favorite foods and music and movies. I've spent more time at her bedside than in my own bed, giving up my life for hers. Everyone thinks she's lost her identity, but so have I."

"You didn't answer my question," I said quietly.

Stacey brushed away a swarm of gnats. "No, I don't hate her. I hate what she became."

"Personality changes caused by a brain injury aren't necessarily—"

"*Became*," she cut in sharply. "The Alex I knew disappeared long before the accident."

"Something happened to her before she crashed?"

"You could say that," she replied, her voice hoarse.

"What?"

"Ask her."

"She doesn't have any recollection—"

"How handy for her to rub out who she was and what she did."

"It won't do any good for me to ask, if—"

"Ask Alex," Stacey said bitterly. "Ask her why we broke up a month *before* the accident."

"*Was*," Alex said an hour later. "Stacey *was* my partner."

I'd driven straight from the park to Sinclair Rehabilitation Center. "Yes."

"*Was*. For all those years, but no longer. *Was*. Do traumatic events impact relationships, or do traumatic relationships impact events?"

"I'm not sure I'm following you," I said hesitantly. "Is it okay if I open the window?"

From her seat on a padded, straightback chair, she nodded, then resumed stretching her right leg.

Alex's room, a twelve-by-twelve square, was decorated with white paint and industrial mauve carpet. A vase of fresh-cut daisies sat on a small round table in the corner of the room. A corkboard hung on the wall near the door, a monthly calendar of activities at Sinclair and a list of channels for the ceiling-mounted television pinned to it.

I slid open the large window that looked out over a grassy common area, closed the door to the bathroom and rested against Alex's unmade bed. "That's better."

"Stacey and I, we split in two before my accident?"

I nodded. "According to her, a month before."

Alex glanced toward the nightstand to a framed, contemporary photograph of her and Stacey, which she'd covered in Post-it notes. "I've wondered about that."

"Do you remember why you broke up?"

With each leg extension, she clutched her thigh. "I had a dream last night."

"Did you write it down?"

"That wasn't necessary. I couldn't forget if I tried. Nothing hurt."

"Excuse me?"

"Nothing was broken or twisted, bruised or severed. I was whole again."

"Does the dream relate to Stacey?"

"I'm not sure." Her breathing became more shallow. "Am I attractive?"

"Yes," I said, looking past her uncombed hair, baggy sweats and loose-hanging sweatshirt. "Very."

Alex stared at me keenly. "Are you attracted to me?"

"I'm in a relationship."

She flashed an enigmatic smile. "Does that matter?"

"To me, yes. To my partner, Destiny, I hope."

"Why did I hire you?"

"To help you get your life back."

Her eyes widened, and she whispered loudly, "What if I don't want it back?"

They think I can't remember, but I can.
On the drive to meet her, my self-hatred had reached new heights.
How could I have begun at Juilliard and ended on Federal

Boulevard?

I stopped by a coffeehouse this morning, and on the register, someone had taped the verse, "Would the child you were be proud of the adult you've become?" The words mocked me for hours. Every time I erased them from my memory, they circled back more violently.

I wanted to believe there was a way out of this life, some joy to be found in the vortex between birth and death, but I had little confidence.

For the moment, I coped.

I pulled into Henny's Used Cars for an appointment with Henrietta "Henny" Carmichael. I'd seen her on late-night television ads, but they'd done little to prepare me for her presence. I was overwhelmed by her girth, her sharp-toed cowboy boots and her body odor mixed with perfume. She crushed my hand in friendliness, slapped me on the back and led me to her office.

This meeting was no different than others I'd conducted over the course of my advertising career, but for some reason, it felt different.

I offered my best ideas, and Henny dismissed them.

I served up mediocre alternatives, and she embraced them.

I couldn't believe that this was what I contributed to the world on a daily basis, but I plodded on.

"We can build the campaign around no haggling," I suggested.

"They'd never believe that. A used-car dealer not haggling? Get real, Alex. Truth be told, I love to make customers sweat. It's the best part of the business."

"A special car-buying service for women? Emphasize that you treat them with respect?"

"People are sick of that bullshit," she said. "Honestly, chicks should have to work just as hard for it. No special favors . . . I screw them all!"

I tried not to frown at her cackling. "Could we highlight your great service department?"

She gestured toward the three-bay area. "Great for me, maybe. Candidly, the real reason I sell cars is so I can fix them."

"Could I build the jingles around your solid reputation?"

"Last I checked, I didn't have one, so that would be false advertising, wouldn't it?"

I shocked myself by saying, "I give up."

Henny waved. "A smart lady like you, and you don't have any ideas?"

I willed myself to speak. "How about playing up your inventory?"

"No can do. Between you and me, I run it lean and mean, which makes this a money machine."

Her rhyme triggered one from me. "How about structuring it around Henny and a penny? That you'll help people with financing?"

She slapped her thigh. "Now you're talking. There's nothing better in the business than high-interest loans."

"I'd create variations on the ads, but all of them could end with something like 'Just got a penny, ask for Henny.'"

She jumped from her chair, embarrassing me with her excitement. "You have talent. Let's hear some openings."

I extracted a pad from my briefcase, blocked out the sound of Henny's uneven breathing and wrote for several minutes.

I'd played in the most venerable concert halls in the world, under the direction of the most demanding conductors, in front of the most discerning audiences.

This wasn't pressure.

When I finished jotting, I read her samples. "Walking to work hurting your stride? Time to get your own ride. Need to get around town, but no money down? Never fear, no payments till next year. It won't take a dime, more like a penny. Come on in and ask for Henny."

I stopped speaking, because I felt dizzy, but Henny Carmichael looked giddy.

She pulled out a check and signed it for an obscene amount.

When she crumpled my hand as we parted, I plastered a smile on my face, but less than a block from the dealership, I had to pull to the side of the road to throw up.

Was I sick from the truth or the lies?

I couldn't begin to know anymore.

CHAPTER 4

"Alex!" I said loudly.

She shook her head as if to clear it and resumed expanding and contracting muscles in her leg. "I'm sorry. I didn't hear what you said."

"If you don't want to continue, we can stop."

"At any point?"

"Whenever you want."

She cocked her head. "Have you ever hated your work?"

"At times. Not this job," I added hastily. "My last one. I owned a marketing firm."

"Did you hate yourself for going to work?"

"Some days. Do you remember much about your job?"

"No."

"According to Stacey, you were a successful jingle writer. You wrote lyrics and music for radio and television ads. Catchy songs that made people want to buy products or services."

"What type of products or services?"

"Cars. Legal representation. Furniture."

"What a strange preoccupation," she mused. "How did I come upon it?"

"When you were younger, you played the piano."

"Competently?"

"You were extremely gifted. When you were in your teens, you performed around the world."

"I've seen the world? All of it?"

I laughed. "Not all of it, but more than most people manage."

"Why did it feel so small?"

"You remember that?"

"Vaguely. My small world."

"Do you remember Juilliard?"

"A friend?" she said, her face flushed.

"A prestigious music school. You attended on full scholarship."

"Juilliard. That's how I came to write jingles?"

"Not directly. You dropped out and held an assortment of odd jobs, none of which you liked. About five years ago, one of your father's friends who owns an ad agency hired you for a freelance project. Shortly after, you started your own business. Evidently, you were good at what you did and well-compensated. You made as much as five thousand dollars at a time for a few hours of work."

"Is that a lot?"

"Most people would be grateful to earn that much in a month. Stacey says you're rich."

"*I'm* rich. Not we? Stacey and I don't share money?"

"No."

Alex looked confused. "Does money matter?"

"To almost everyone."

"Why?"

"As a marker of success. For security. Oh, hell," I said, frustrated, "I don't know."

She smiled broadly. "Do you need some?"

"Thanks, but I have enough."

"If I made a lot of money in such a short amount of time, how did I spend my free hours? What did I do to myself? Who did it with me?"

They think I can't remember, but I can.

I met his mother before I met him.

For sixty days that summer, no rain had fallen on Denver, and when the skies finally opened, the clouds released a long-held wrath. The volume of water, heavy winds and lightning crippled the city, and our neighborhood took the brunt of it, elms and cottonwoods splitting and falling on every block.

In the middle of the nighttime thunderstorm, she and I came racing out of our houses when a transformer across the alley blew. After hurried introductions, she helped remove a limb from the top of my car, and I helped bail water out of her basement.

Because her son was with his father and Stacey was at work, my neighbor and I battled the storm alone, spending most of the night restoring order.

The next day, she sent her only child to my aid, and he rang the doorbell, which I ignored. Only after he knocked for several minutes did I come to the security door.

He held a saw, rake and handful of Hefty bags. "Ma'am, you should fix your doorbell."

"I'm not interested," I said, my response to all solicitations.

"Mama told me to come clean your yard."

"Dianna sent you?" I replied, seconds late in making the connection. He shared her smooth skin, although his was several shades darker, and his eyes were identical, oversized saucers. His hair looked like hers, tight knots cut close to the scalp. "You must be Derek."

"Yes, ma'am."

"I'm Alex. You can stop calling me ma'am."

"Mama says I have to show respect."

"Respect is fine, but if someone asks you to stop, you should honor the request."

"Yes, ma—"

"Call me Alex."

"Yes, Alex."

"How much do you charge?"

"What?"

I gestured toward the tangle of branches on the front lawn. "For your services."

"Oh," he said, comprehending. "Mama said I can't accept money, even if you try to make me. She said if I come home with any, she'll march me right over to give it back."

I smiled. "She wouldn't begrudge you a refreshment, would she?"

His forehead scrunched in confusion. "What?"

"How about a pop? Coke, root beer, cream soda?"

He lit up. "Root beer."

He drank his first soda out of a bottle, and we spent the rest of the afternoon together.

The next day, he returned to help me with chores around the house, and in the weeks that followed, we cleaned out the basement and garage and fixed the toilet and garage door. We painted porches, extended gutters, replanted patches of lawn and trimmed hedges.

Routine jobs came alive as I taught and he learned, absorbing everything at rapid speed, extrapolating concepts to new dimensions.

I told Dianna that he was bright beyond our reach.

One day, she suggested I teach Derek how to play the piano. I agreed, instantly regretting the promise. After our first session, he declared that he hated picking for sounds on wooden keys, and we dropped the lessons.

He did, however, enjoy the jingles I concocted. They fascinated him, and he pleaded to join me in my afternoon sessions in the studio. I capped his time at one hour per day, but soon his imprint was on everything I sold. He delighted at rhyming, and his inquisitive mind pushed mine to higher levels. We were a productive team, he and I, but our most lucrative achievement embarrassed me.

"Turn your crash into cash" was exclusively his creation.

He spoke the ditty and hummed the music for the personal injury law firm. I simply documented the text and notes, sold the campaign to the client and set up an account in his name, seeding it with the first $1,000 royalty check. Dianna protested, but she knew her job as an administrative assistant would never provide enough to send Derek to

*college, and her ex-husband drank more than he made. Stacey chided me
for "paying off a kid," but I overlooked her pettiness. I invited her to join
in our weekly Risk battles, but she had no patience for games or children.
Instead, Derek and I roped in Dianna or matched wits at chess.*

He had no other friends, and neither did I.

Yet I never considered what we'd do without each other.

"How do you know so much about me and what I did?" Alex said
after a long silence. She eyed me with suspicion. "I led a complicated
life, more than one life. No one knew me."

"You asked me to help recover your memories, and Stacey told
me about your jingle writing. She also gave me a box of work-related
materials from your freelance business. I'll bring it with me next
time, and we can look through it. A few minutes ago, when you
drifted off, you said the word *Henny*. Is that Henny Carmichael, the
car dealer?"

"Henny?"

"She was one of your clients. I could call and invite her to visit.
Would you like that?"

Alex became still. "I don't know what I like anymore."

"Yesterday when I was here, you also asked about someone
named Derek. Stacey told me he's a boy who used to live down
the street from you. I tried calling his mother, but the phone's been
disconnected. I can drop by and see them in the next few days. How
does that sound?"

"Do what you have to do." Alex took a deep breath and exhaled
suddenly. "I feel an urgency to remember, a life-and-death pull."

"Why?"

"Have you seen my medical file? Do you know about the
crash?"

"I haven't seen any medical records, but I know you were in a
single-car accident, a roll-over."

Blotches formed on her face. "Would a seatbelt have prevented
my injuries?"

"I don't know. Do you remember not wearing one?"

"Stacey told me," she said, her leg twitching. "The injuries are my fault."

"A belt might have made a difference, but accidents happen."

"I always wore a belt."

I looked at her with concern. "In terms of memory, is there something specific you'd like to remember?"

On the verge of tears, she said, "I don't know."

"Or forget?"

She nodded faintly. "Maybe."

"Can you talk about it?"

She shook her head in slow motion. "Not yet."

"Are you okay? Are you in pain?"

Alex covered her mouth with a trembling hand. "Always."

I rose. "Should I get a nurse?"

She grabbed my arm, startling me with the strength of her grip. "Is it possible I tried to kill myself?"

Was it possible that Alex Madigen had attempted suicide using a four thousand–pound weapon?

Good question, one that I contemplated as I drove like a granny back to the office.

Had Alex's crash been a mere accident, a mishap that could have happened to anyone, reckless driving, a careless act on the part of someone who was beyond caring, or an intentional move, a deliberate desire to end her life on August sixteenth? I had a few ideas about how to find the answer, but they fell out of my head as soon as I saw Fran Green standing on the sidewalk outside our office.

I screeched to a halt and jumped out of the car. "I told you to do one thing. Interview Henny Carmichael about her relationship with Alex Madigen."

Fran wiggled her finger for me to come closer. "You'll fall in love."

My hands clutched my head. "I don't want to fall in love."

"Sleek and shapely, isn't she?"

"You did *not* buy a new car," I shouted.

"Might have," she said, nonplussed. "Used, not new, which is why Henny's offering us a deal."

"Us?"

"Company car. We share and trade off every other week. Only been driven seven hundred miles, by VIPs at a golf tourney. Still smells new."

I groaned. "Tell me you didn't do this."

"Might have. Not sure what I signed. Who can read those contracts, with the gray ink and four-point type? Check it out." Fran caressed the roof of the Lexus LS 430.

"I am *not* getting in."

"One spin around the block. Have to experience the ride. Smooth as can be. Makes the world disappear. And the kick, don't get me started. Had to keep my eye on the speedometer. Barely tapped the accelerator, and this darling zoomed."

"No!"

"You like the color?"

"Gray? What am I supposed to say?"

"Flint mica, Kris. Get with the program. Feast your eyes on these safety features," she said, bobbing around the car like a schoolgirl. "Airbags, swiveling headlights, backup cameras, mirrors that adjust when you put the car in reverse."

Passing by on one of her rounds, she grabbed my hand, but I yanked it back. "No!"

"Climate-controlled seats. Fans circulate chilled air on your rear."

"Chilled air?" I said meekly.

Fran opened the passenger door and made a swooping gesture. "Right on your rump." I let out a heavy sigh and sat where she pointed, in the front passenger seat, but I left my right leg hanging out of the car. Fran skipped around to the driver's side and hopped in. "See what I mean. Colder than our office. We could hold meetings in this baby. Get WiFi, do our computer work out here."

I leaned back, caressed by the leather. "One thing, Fran! Interview Henny Carmichael. That was it!"

"Had to talk somewhere. Henny suggested the front seat of this honey. Next thing I knew, the engine was on and away we went. Watch." Fran tapped the brake, pushed a knob, and I heard a purr. "No key. Fob in my pocket. Slick, eh?"

"How much?"

She pushed a button on the audio panel, bringing Carly Simon in from the backseat. "Henny threw out a ballpark, fifty-two."

I shot upright, almost hitting my head on the windshield. "Fifty-two thousand dollars?"

"Give or take, but Henny offered me seventy-five hundred for the Ranger. Five-year loan, eight-percent financing. Who can beat it? Maybe we should bump down to the model below this one. Save us six large if we sacrifice the navigation system."

"Six hundred?"

"Six thou. We could rough it. Buy maps, look over our shoulders. Drive the old-fashioned way."

"Fifty-two thousand dollars," I repeated in a small voice, feeling weak. "Do you have any idea what the payments would be on that amount?"

"Didn't get that far. Henny-Penny and me, we're talking specifics later."

"Wait here." Determined, I went into the office and returned a few minutes later with a calculator. "Take fifty-two thousand, add seven-point-six percent for sales tax, subtract seventy-five hundred for the trade-in. Five years, eight percent. This is the payment."

Fran looked at the screen. "Holy crap! I better take this sucker back."

"Today! We're not paying nine hundred and eighty-two dollars a month for a car."

"Supposed to be a one-week test drive. Hope it doesn't get ugly. In the car game, it's all sweetness and light, till someone gets hurt."

"You're probably stuck with the car," I said, relishing the moment.

Fran paled. "No, siree. You come with."

"I'm not going anywhere. You got into this. You get out of it. I'm sure you'll work something out. What was Henny like?"

"Skinnier than on the tube."

"Doesn't the camera add pounds?"

"Might, but our friend Henny had gastric bypass between her last television rollout and this fine day. Wouldn't recommend it. Killed her appetite. Gave her bad breath, too." Fran reached into a cubby behind the stickshift. "Mento?"

"No, thanks."

She popped a candy into her mouth. "Hen made a serious dent in my stash. Had to stop by a Seven-Eleven on the way back. Where was I? Oh, yeah. Throws people for a loop now that she's lost her fat suit." Fran reacted to my sharp exhale. "Her words, not mine. Feels like she took a shortcut and lost her way. That's besides the thirty-K she forked over for the operation. Know how she gained weight?"

"I can't imagine how this relates to—"

"Two pounds a year. Doesn't sound like much, but use your H-P calculator and add it up. Twenty pounds a decade. Better watch out, kiddo. These are your prime gaining years. Me, I survived the high-risk period without a glitch."

I looked over at her roll. "Not exactly."

Fran patted her stomach affectionately. "Insurance, in case I get lost in the woods. Nothing health-threatening. Barely noticeable. You want the temperature adjusted in your side of the cabin?"

"No."

"Be cooler if you'd shut the door."

I glared at her, and she shrugged.

"Suit yourself. Know what Henny's favorite foods are?"

"How does this apply to our case?"

"Bagels, Cheetos and chocolates. Who's that remind you of?"

"*You* are irritating me."

"I can see that," she said jovially. "Your face is all red. With you having the same food interests, that might be cause for alarm."

"I don't care what size Henny Carmichael is or how she gained or lost weight. Could you please just tell me what she thought of Alex Madigen?"

"No need to scream." Fran moved her seat farther back, into a more reclined position. She reached into the storage drawer in the padded armrest, pulled out a small spiral notebook, held it at arm's length and peered intensely. "Described our client. Let me get this accurate. Talented. Fast-thinker. Tightly wound. Two hit it off right away. Henny liked Alex's upbeat music and clever wordplay."

"Did Alex ever tell her about her career as a pianist?"

"Apparently, never breathed a word. Kept it to herself that she was a child prodigy. Henny wouldn't have cared anyhow. Wasn't looking for Mozart. Needed someone to come up with a campaign to help sell cars. Which, our Alex did when she was on top of her game. Turned work in on time and dug the process, but the honeymoon didn't last."

"What changed?"

"Sometime in their second year of working together, our whiz showed up late to meetings, looking scruffy, couldn't keep her eye on the ball. Zoned out, middle of sentences, acted like a zombie."

"Was she on drugs or alcohol?"

"Asked the same question, but our friendly car dealer couldn't say. Did notice the behavior worsened. Alex started canceling meetings, never rescheduled. Stopped returning calls, missed deadlines."

I fiddled with the door lock. "This isn't good."

"I'm only the messenger." Fran plucked a check from the back of the notebook. "Speaking of which, Henny asked me to deliver this."

"What's it for?" I said, raising an eyebrow at the sum of $2,500.

"Reissue of one of Alex's checks. Girl never cashed the original."

"Did you talk to Henny about visiting Alex?"

"Yep and nope. Won't do it. Not good in hospitals."

"Alex is in a rehab center."

"Doesn't like those either."

"No one does."

"Henny nursed her mum through a long illness. Won't go near any type of institution. Ain't gonna happen."

"Damn it."

"Deals-On-Wheels probably wasn't the best choice for a first visitor anyway. Those two weren't on what you'd call friendly terms."

"Why?"

"Henny fired our virtuoso." Fran palmed two more candies and shoved them into her mouth. "Two months before the big crash. Hated to, but had no choice."

CHAPTER 5

Henny Carmichael had fired Alex Madigen in June, Alex and Stacey Wilhite had broken up in July, and Alex had rolled her car in August.

No wonder my client wasn't sure she wanted her life back, particularly if something worse had precipitated those two events leading up to the crash.

I would have liked to have taken the next steps in the case, but Fran convinced me to spend the rest of the afternoon and most of the next day prepping for my first decoy assignment—a giant waste of time in my mind.

The moment Fran left the office Wednesday evening, I tried to block out all thoughts of betrayal, but glimpses of what lay ahead continued to intrude, making me feel queasy.

I chose Mexican food as a solution for indigestion, and carrying a burrito the size of a small football, I arrived home a few minutes after seven, parked in my space off the alley and climbed the back stairs of the mansion I co-owned with Destiny. Located on Gaylord Street, in Denver's historic Capitol Hill district, the 1905 Queen Anne Victorian was separated into three units, one per floor, with a laundry and workout room in the basement.

Once inside our top-floor apartment, to create the impression of company, I turned on the TV and all the lights. I changed into shorts and a tank top and debated whether to eat or exercise. I could have benefited from a round of weight training, but it seemed like too much work to get to the workout room. Instead, I cut the burrito in two pieces, refrigerated one and ate the other from a paper towel, spraying black beans and rice across couch cushions in the living room.

For mindless hours, I watched television, flipping around until ten, when I ate two root beer popsicles, caught the top of the local news and then went to bed.

But not to sleep.

Lying in the middle of the queen-sized bed I normally shared with Destiny, my thoughts finally shifted from Roxanne Herbert and Linda Palizzi, my decoy client and target, to Alex Madigen and her loss of identity.

What defined us anyway?

Relationships and roles? Income and career? Personality and values? Plans and achievements? Desires and deeds?

Which was it?

All, some or none of the above?

If everything vanished, what would remain? Could a core part of our beings continue to exist in the absence of anything tangible?

On behalf of Alex Madigen, I was about to find out.

Wednesday night, I barely slept, yet somehow, Thursday at noon came all too soon.

"I'm not sure this is a good idea," Roxanne Herbert said a few minutes after twelve.

"No problem," I replied easily. "There's no charge for the initial consultation. After I outline our decoy services, if you don't feel comfortable, I'll leave. If we agree to proceed, you can call it off at any point. You're in control."

"That'd be a first."

"What made you call Test-A-Mate?"

She stood and began to pace. "I'm not sure."

Aware of her every step echoing on the gleaming hardwood floors, I glanced around the living room of the Tudor house. The meticulousness of the inside—fresh ivory paint, immaculate woodwork, Crate and Barrel furnishings—matched the outside of the property, but not the neighborhood. The home was situated on a dicey block in northwest Denver, and even though the property had been improved with xeriscaping, a wrought iron fence and a flagstone walkway, the neighbors hadn't followed suit. One adjoining lot had a disabled car in the side yard, the other a mattress on the front porch of the house, and those were the more positive features.

Roxanne paused in front of a wall of photographs, a collection of high-quality, matted images of her and Linda Palizzi in happier times. "Something's changed with Linda."

"Recently?"

She lowered herself to the loveseat across from me. "Gradually, over the last few years."

"How long have you and your—?" I broke off. "Do you prefer wife, girlfriend, lover, partner?"

"Life partner. We've been together ten years, if that's what you were about to ask. Linda and I met in college."

I took out a notepad and uncapped a pen. "Have you noticed a variation in her habits?"

"I'm not sure." Roxanne used French manicured nails to tug at a loose thread on the pocket of her black jacket. She wore matching trousers, a maroon silk shirt, gray scarf and gold hoop earrings. At unpredictable intervals, she squinted, but only with her right eye.

"Have there been any unexplained charges on Linda's credit card?"

"I never see the bill. We have separate accounts."

"Phone calls at odd hours?"

"She always gets those. She's in charge of cadaver donations at

Park Hospital. When donors die, their families call to make arrangements."

I made a note and looked up again. "Has Linda changed her hairstyle or wardrobe?"

"No."

"Bought new underpants or bras?"

Roxanne's face reddened. "About a month ago, Linda threw away everything in her underwear drawer and started over. Is that a bad sign?"

The worst. Spouses never hesitated to subject loved ones to all varieties of stained and tattered undergarments, but as soon as they began to troll, out came the fresh whiteys, according to the gospel of Fran Green. "Not necessarily," I said mildly. "Let's take it one step at a time. Nothing strikes you as unusual in her movements, nothing at all?"

After a long pause, Roxanne mumbled, "She does go to the gym a lot. Two or three times a week."

"That's not uncommon."

"For three or four hours at a time."

I whistled softly. "Does she look more fit?"

Roxanne shrugged. "I can't tell."

"That's what aroused your suspicion?"

"Partially."

"Something else?"

"Linda's always noticed other women. She'll comment on how beautiful they are. Their shoulders, or legs or eyes. I've asked her to stop, but she won't. She doesn't mean anything by it, and she says she'd never act on it, but I'm not so sure. Sometimes at parties, she gives a woman a compliment while I'm standing there, as if she doesn't see me anymore."

I nodded sympathetically. "And this has become worse lately?"

"Much. Linda keeps forming intense attachments to women, one at a time. She'll talk about them incessantly. It's hard to explain, but she's just . . . different." Roxanne paused. "I was laid off at the beginning of last year. For the past seventeen months, I've been looking for a job, but I can't find anything suitable."

"I'm sorry to hear that," I said, not having the courage to share that two inches of black roots showing through blond hair might affect chances for employment.

She picked at the sleeve of her jacket. "I was an executive at Qwest. The first three months after they fired me, I looked for work every day, then less and less. But I have an interview this afternoon."

"That's encouraging."

"My first this year, for temp work. I had to buy a new suit. None of my clothes fit anymore," she said, gesturing to her waistline. "Some days, it's all I can do to get out of bed."

"Maybe this will—"

"I started taking antidepressants, but they make me jumpy. I can't sleep. I have no sex drive. Maybe that's why . . ." Her voice faded glumly.

I cleared my throat. "What if we—"

"I don't know what else to do," she blurted out, bursting into tears.

I handed Roxanne a tissue from the pack Fran had stuffed into my binder during our practice session. "You have to trust your instincts. Something prompted you to make the call. Whatever the outcome, wouldn't you rather know the truth?"

She sniffled. "Can there be a good outcome?"

"Sometimes," I said, a lie. One hundred percent of the time, when a spouse footed the bill for surveillance or decoy, Fran's instructor had informed his students, the agency exposed a cheater.

Roxanne wadded up the tissue. "How much does it cost?"

"Three hundred dollars per meeting."

"How many meetings will it take?"

"That depends." With male targets, two at the most. With female targets, who knew? Fran's trainer hadn't had any experience with woman-to-woman cases. "Probably no more than three."

Roxanne's face twisted. "Do I have to introduce you to Linda?"

"No, no," I said quickly. "I'll bump into her. How about at the gym?"

"She pulled an abdominal muscle, and she can't lift weights or do cardio for a month."

"Does she frequent a particular bar or nightclub?"

"She better not. She's a recovering alcoholic."

"Any volunteer work?"

"No, but I have an idea. Do you know anyone who has a body to donate?"

I shivered. "A dead person?"

"Or alive. People decide ahead of time to donate their bodies to science."

Too creepy. I shook my head. "Linda goes to work and exercises? Nothing else?"

"Sometimes she puts in time at the rental property we own." Roxanne sat up straight. "She's been over at the house in Bonnie Brae every night this week. We have a vacancy, and she's running an ad starting on Sunday."

"Let's go that route. I'll pose as a prospective tenant and call her next week."

"Then what?"

"We'll see what happens. I'll carry a hidden tape recorder, and after my meeting with Linda, you can come by our office and pick up a copy of the tape."

"You won't have sex with her?"

"Absolutely not. We have a strict code of ethics. I won't flirt, and I won't make or respond to physical overtures. Linda will have to initiate, and if her behavior crosses the line, I'll shut it down."

Roxanne fixed me with a flinty stare. "What if you're attracted to her?"

"I won't be. This is a business transaction."

"You've had experience? You'll know what to do?"

"Most assuredly." I pulled out a one-page, Test-A-Mate contract, the one Fran had designed the day before, and handed it to Roxanne. "If you're not ready to make a decision yet, I'll leave this with you, and you can think it over."

Roxanne leaned forward and snatched the pen out of my hand. "All I've been doing is thinking. I need to move on with my life."

And that was that.

With her signature, Roxanne Herbert started something she

couldn't stop if she tried. If her life partner fell for the bait, she'd have irrefutable evidence that their relationship had disintegrated. If Linda didn't succumb to temptation, Roxanne would have to live with her own treachery.

Either way, their lives would never be the same.

To take my mind off cheating, I went home, changed into running clothes and completed two laps around Cheesman Park. Three miles later, my edgy feelings about Roxanne Herbert, Linda Palizzi and the Test-A-Mate business had subsided only slightly.

I returned home, changed back into a blue and white pinstripe button-down, blue flare-leg pants and black loafers and rushed to make my three o'clock appointment with Alex Madigen at Sinclair Rehabilitation Center.

I found Alex in her room, positioned in the middle of her neatly made bed, one leg crossed over the other. Surrounded by dozens of books, most of which she'd propped open, she was bent over, writing on a pad. All of the reminder notes in the room had disappeared, as well as the photo of her and Stacey.

At my knock, she paused, looked up and broke into a smile. "Kris, come in."

"You look busy."

"Kelly drove me to the bookstore yesterday."

"Ah!" I set a box on the table, walked toward her and picked up a book. "*Hottest Careers In America*. Are you trying to figure out what you want to be when you grow up?"

"Yes, and I have the answer. Happy."

"Does that pay well?" I said, laughing with her.

"Extremely."

I perched on the edge of the bed, and she moved books to make room for me. "Do you think you'll return to music?"

"I'm not sure. When I was a child, the decision was made for me. This time, I prefer to live more deliberately."

"Why did you quit playing the piano? Can you remember that?"

"My mother thinks I can't, but I can." Alex pinched the bridge of her nose. "I longed for something more from music, something I never found easy to attain. From the day I began to play, I was told I had a gift, but I came to despise myself for the sounds I made."

"You hated the piano?"

"I did. I craved silence, and I didn't play for years. Not until . . . shortly before my accident."

"Could you go back to playing professionally? Is that one of your career possibilities?"

"Perhaps. When I play now, the sensations feel new, as if I'm once again discovering the wonder. Oddly, I'm as proficient as ever. That part of my brain appears unaffected by the trauma."

"That's fortunate."

"I suppose it is." She flashed a wan smile. "I've begun to feel as if I can contribute something meaningful, but it may be a while before I regain full function. I'm working on balance issues, short-term and long-term memory, walking without a limp, pain management."

"Are you on pain meds?"

She frowned. "Nothing stronger than Advil. Two weeks ago, I went off Oxycontin because I couldn't focus on anything except the next pill. Pain, as difficult as it is to endure, feels better than numbness. I don't trust myself with mind-altering options. I never have."

"Were you addicted to something before the accident? Alcohol or drugs?"

She shook her head firmly. "Never those. I remember being careful. I knew if I found a way to mute my feelings, I wouldn't ever be able to stop."

I pointed to a small poster pinned to the bulletin board. "Is that new?"

Her features softened. "It is. I made it last night on the computer. Five goals to attain in the next year. Live independently. Stay in the moment. Give piano lessons. Make friends. Go on a real date."

"What's a real date?"

"In public, and I want it to end with a kiss."

"Just a kiss?"

"Not necessarily."

Alex cast a furtive glance at me, and I coughed nervously. "You could return to work gradually, couldn't you? A few hours a week."

"Possibly. They think I can lead a normal life, but I can't."

"Why?"

"I'm at increased risk for seizures, Parkinson's and depression."

"How much risk—"

She talked over me. "Arthritis will set in, and undoubtedly, I'll need a hip replacement. At all cost, I must avoid another brain injury. Dangerous activities are strictly prohibited."

"That rules out skydiving and boxing," I said lightly.

Alex replied in a serious tone, "I've already lost nine months of my life, and my second chance is only half a chance."

"Still, it's a chance."

"The standard goal of rehabilitation is to return to one's previous occupation, but I refuse."

"No more jingle writing. Why?"

Her face went slack. "Because every time I sold something, it felt like a defeat."

"You've remembered that?"

"Mmm," she said despondently.

"Then maybe we don't need to look through this," I said, moving toward the table, where I opened the top flaps of the box I'd carried in from the car.

"What is it?"

"Work-related materials from your freelance business. Stacey gave it to me when we met on Tuesday. She said you'd cleaned out your studio shortly before the accident."

Her eyes flickered. "One box? That's all I kept? Have you looked inside?"

"Not yet. Should we do it together?"

Alex flung back her head. "Search if you'd like. I prefer to read my books."

"Okay." I unloaded everything onto the table and began to study the paperwork. I shuffled through contracts, lyrics, sheets of music, invoices and balance sheets.

An hour into the task, just as I was about to open an envelope of sales tax records, Alex spoke up. "The pieces of my life that lie on the table, what do they tell you about me?"

I pushed back my chair. "You had a successful business, that's obvious."

"Is it?"

"Yes, but your work came to a virtual standstill about two to three months before your accident."

She gave me a peculiar look. "You can tell this from the box?"

"And from an interview earlier this week with Henny Carmichael."

"Henny?"

"The car dealer who was one of your biggest clients. Apparently, she dropped you."

"Did she?" Alex said nonchalantly. "Why?"

"Henny claims you frequently canceled meetings, then stopped showing up altogether."

"I must have been preoccupied with something." Alex waved airily. "I assume she won't be visiting me?"

"No, but she sent a royalty check for twenty-five hundred dollars, a replacement for one you never deposited."

"Payment in full when I didn't cash out?"

I smiled. "Something like that. Do you want me to bring it to you, or should I give it to Stacey?"

"Stacey, please. I'm not ready to handle finances." Alex wiped her forehead with the back of her hand. "Henny Carmichael won't enter the halls of Sinclair. Will anyone come?"

"Hopefully, Derek Wallace, your young friend, will come with his mother, Dianna. I can tell from some of your work notes and payments you made to him that he helped with the jingles. Do you remember anything about your creative process?"

Without warning, she cowered. "No."

Concerned, I looked at her. "Stacey gave me an address for the Wallaces, and I stopped by their house yesterday, but they've moved. I should be able to track them down through a public records data company. Are you sure you still want to see Derek?"

"I must have," Alex said hazily, "or I wouldn't have tried so hard."

"To remember?"

Her breath quickened. "To forget."

"What do you mean?"

"I've got to go," she gasped, running for the bathroom.

They think I can't remember, but I can.

The precise second the call came in.

Derek and Dianna were camping in the mountains, and I was in their apartment watering their plants.

At first, I didn't recognize the number on my cell phone or her distorted voice, but I heard the words clearly. "Derek has passed."

I fell to the floor and whispered, "That isn't possible."

"The current was too much," Dianna said. "His heart stopped."

Unable to make a sound, I clenched my fists and scraped them against the carpet. Dianna continued to speak slowly, exposing details that couldn't be real, and I crawled into Derek's race car bed and clutched his sheets. For as many moments as I could bear, I needed to lay there, in this last place he lay.

I had no idea how I would go on but knew that I must.

I had to be strong for Dianna.

I suppressed my tears through the call and past the funeral, but delaying only increased the severity, and when at last I cried, I couldn't stop.

Try as I did, I couldn't stop missing him . . . the boy who came too late and left too soon.

CHAPTER 6

Alex didn't make it to the toilet in time, which set in motion a sequence of events.

I pressed the call button, and a nurse came in to check on her, followed by an aide tasked with cleaning up the trail of vomit and helping Alex change out of her tunic and stretch pants. I hurriedly packed up the contents of the box of business materials, escaping before I retched.

Hours later, I still felt shaken.

I gave myself the next day off, beginning a long weekend, during which, with Destiny absent, I acted in ways I was ashamed to say.

Friday night, I ate cereal for dinner and fell asleep in front of the television without brushing my teeth.

Saturday, I turned the air conditioner on high, just because I could, and pushed a couch down the alley, removing it from the edge of our property, foisting it onto others. I overcooked a batch of Rice Krispies bars and ate the caramelized monstrosities in bed.

Sunday, I made believe I wasn't home when the downstairs renters came calling for a donation to their latest cause and killed flies
and spiders and ants inside the house. Slayings, in Destiny's estima-
tion. I put the backyard birds on a diet, one cup of seed per day, not
three, and only flushed after every second pee. I didn't wash or comb
my hair all day.

By Monday, I was relieved to return to the office.

"Never guess who came by the house yesterday," Fran greeted me
boisterously, before I could shut the front door. "Don't even try. The
sisters."

"From your convent?"

"Don't I wish? Nope, those sisters act like I died, letting a little
issue like homosexuality muddy our friendship. These were sisters
from the local church."

I took a seat at my desk. "Jehovah's Witnesses?"

"None other. Two well-dressed ladies came to talk about the
discouraging news. Thought they meant the city council election.
Finally, someone here to address the issues we been having in the
alley. Graffiti, buggies, druggies, illegal dumping. Then it dawned on
me they meant the discouraging news in the world, sure to be fixed
with Christ-cramming."

"Were you wearing that shirt?" I said, referencing the black letter-
ing on neon yellow fabric, *Proud To Be An American Lesbian*.

"Nah. Had on *One In Ten, You Do The Math*. Might have gone
over their heads."

I leaned back in my chair. "You should never answer the door
when you're not expecting visitors."

"Ain't that the truth! No good comes from it. But enough about
my weekend. How's the amnesiac?"

"Don't call Alex that."

"You ask her the three most important questions, the ones I gave
you last week?"

"No, Fran."

"First love? First lay? First lie? That'd speed things up."

I shot her a fake smile. "Thanks for your help."

"Anytime. Anything else I can do for you?"

"Seriously?"

"Need something to keep me busy or I'll have to wash the sidewalk again."

"I need a current address or place of employment for a Dianna Wallace. She and her son, Derek, used to live down the street from Alex, but they've moved."

Fran made a note on her blotter. "Check."

"Also, do you still have that contact at the highway patrol department?"

"Yep. Met for ice cream last week."

"Could you get in touch with her and find out what you can about Alex's accident? We need to read the accident report or talk to someone who worked the scene."

"Done. Looking for anything specific?"

"Stacey told Alex she wasn't wearing a seatbelt, and Alex is afraid she might have tried to kill herself."

Fran blew air out of her cheeks. "Not the first memory you want to recover."

"No kidding! They have a strange relationship, almost adversarial. Stacey's convinced Alex knows more than she's revealing. She believes her memory comes and goes when it's convenient."

"You agree?"

I scrunched up my face and thought about it. "It's not that simple. Essentially, Stacey's accusing her of lying, but I wouldn't go that far. I'd guess pieces are coming back to Alex, and she's afraid to talk about them. She knows more than she's saying, but I can't tell how much. One minute she remembers something, the next she doesn't. I'm getting a lot of double messages."

"Stop you right there," Fran said. "Share one of my favorite Greenisms with you. You ready for it?"

"No, but I'm sure you'll tell me anyway."

She grinned. "Double message—one's a lie."

"That's it?"

"Deeper than you think," she said solemnly, spitting her gum into a Post-it note. "Ouch. Just gave myself a paper cut."

"Are you all right?"

She looked at her reflection in the putter she kept under her desk. "No blood. I'll live. Where was I?"

"Lies."

"Yes, ma'am. Tell your pianist she needs to keep a lie log. Started one myself when the short-term memory deficiencies threatened to endanger the long-term goals."

I raised one eyebrow. "A lie log?"

"Spiral notebook, pocket-size for easy transport. Filled heaps of 'em with the lies I told Ruth. 'Yes, you look good in curlers. No, I don't dislike your mother.' Exhausting, trying to remember all the fibs and fabrications. Much easier this way. Frees the brain for more worthy endeavors." Fran pulled her lower lip to its farthest extension, studied it with her left eye and said in a garbled tone, "Would recommend a separate catalog for the lies she tells herself. Did that for a while, toward the end of the Ruth era."

"You lied to yourself?" I said, not sure I'd understood her.

Fran released her lip and said distinctly, "Don't we all? Can't lie to yourself, who can you lie to?"

Fran spent the better part of the morning tracking down Dianna Wallace's address, paying a small fortune, at twenty-five cents a click, to one of the online database companies we used regularly. She sorted through hundreds of Wallaces across the metro area, with their various current and last known addresses and present and previous employers, before coming up with a single line of useful information.

Once she handed me the slip of paper, I wasted no time in driving to an address in the Five Points neighborhood, a few blocks north of Denver's downtown core.

Grateful that I hadn't taken Fran up on her offer to use the Lexus, I parked on the street across from a three-story apartment building, glanced at units on the second floor and debated whether it was safe to get out of my Honda.

In blinding daylight.

Eventually I convinced myself that if a single mom and her young son felt safe passing by homeless people and drug dealers to enter and exit their building every day, I could do it once.

As a precaution, however, I called Fran and told her where I was and when I would touch base again.

I entered the building, slipping behind a middle-aged man who was too strung out to care that I hadn't used the intercom and buzzer. On the second floor, I knocked on the door to the Wallace residence but received no answer. I wondered if Dianna might be at work, then heard the obvious sound of shuffling feet.

"Dianna, I'm Kristin Ashe. I was wondering if I could talk to you about your son Derek."

"Go away. Whatever you're selling, I'm not buying."

"Stacey Wilhite gave me your name."

"Who?"

"Alex Madigen's partner."

The door opened a crack. "You better come in. I don't need everyone hearing my business."

Dianna Wallace stepped aside, and I gently pushed open the door, a little afraid of what I'd find on the other side. I paused on the three-foot linoleum square that served as an entry, and in semi-darkness, I could make out the gaunt features of a woman in her forties who was dressed in a pink striped T-shirt that dropped to her thighs and white leggings that fit loosely. She had large brown eyes, flawless dark skin and close-cropped hair. She squinted at me through small, black, rectangular glasses before squeezing my hand in a tight grip.

In the small apartment, the shades were drawn and windows closed, and a musty smell hung in the air. The window air-conditioning unit, which was cranking loudly, had done little to cool the room. Days' worth of newspapers were piled in the corner of the living room, dirty dishes were stacked in the kitchen sink, and the furniture looked as if it had arrived in one load from a rent-a-center. No plants, wall hangings, knickknacks or photos were in sight, nor were there any toys, books or games lying around.

"Start over," Dianna said, once we were seated side by side on the couch.

"I'm Kristin Ashe." I set one of my business cards on the coffee table. "I'm a private investigator hired by Alex Madigen. Nine months ago, she was in a horrific car accident."

Dianna's hand flew to her mouth. "I didn't know."

"She was seriously injured, and—"

"How serious?"

"She was thrown from the car and broke her back, her leg and three ribs."

She pressed her hands together, as if in prayer, and shook her head in denial. "No!"

I nodded. "Alex had damage to her liver, but doctors repaired that, and it's healing. The worst trauma, though, was to her head. She took quite a blow."

"Don't tell me—"

"She's functioning, but she has a long road ahead of her."

Dianna's lips tightened. "Such a good woman, so full of love. I did my share of speculating as to why she lost touch, but people do. You can't blame them."

"Alex has very little memory of anything before the accident, and I'm helping her piece together her life. She'll be leaving the rehab center in a few weeks, and she hasn't had many visitors."

"No one called me." Her eyes welled up. "I'll go today. Where's she staying?"

"Sinclair Rehabilitation Center, on Franklin Street, near Saint Luke's Hospital."

"I'll go this afternoon. On my way to work," she said with resolve, before halting abruptly. "Will she know me? Can she see? Can she speak?"

"Her eyesight's perfect, and she can converse. She's lucid most of the time, but she might not recognize you."

"No matter. I'll be there for her."

"Just to prepare you, sometimes she fumbles for words or uses the wrong ones."

Dianna looked at me over the tops of her glasses. "She doesn't have to say anything. She can just be herself."

"She has a short attention span."

"I won't overstay my welcome."

"She goes blank, too. Like she's there, but she's not."

"None of that matters. What does she need?"

"She keeps asking about Derek."

Dianna lit up. "She would. Those two were inseparable."

"You used to live down the street from Alex and Stacey, didn't you?"

She nodded. "Two doors down. That's how we met. Alex was kind enough to help me one night when my basement apartment flooded, and I sent my boy over the next day to clean up her yard. She knew right away what to do with his liveliness. She put him to work, kept his mind and hands busy. He would have spent every minute at her house, if I'd let him. I'd make him come home, so as to give Alex a break."

"What did they do together?"

Dianna laughed, a husky sound. "About everything under the sun. They fixed what they could find in both our houses, until they ran out of chores. She gave Derek a piano lesson, but he didn't take to it. The jingles, though, you couldn't keep him away from those, and Alex paid him," Dianna said proudly. "Some of what they made up, she sold to her customers, and she shared her pay. I wouldn't let him touch the money, but that was neither here nor there for him. From the time he came out of me, that boy was all about noise. Loud, ever so loud."

I laughed with her. "It sounds like they shared something special."

"Oh, yes. Alex was the first person to tell me Derek had potential, that he could be somebody. He talked about her night and day, day and night. Alex this, Alex that." Dianna smiled fondly. "He walked in her light, he did. It hurts my heart to hear this news."

"Alex hasn't died," I said gently. "She's changed, but—"

"No, but nothing will ever be the same. I hear that in what you're telling me. She was a private woman, kept to herself, but I appreciated that she took Derek in and treated him with respect. She was there for both of us in our times of need. I'll do the same."

"Were you serious about visiting this afternoon?"

"I said I would, didn't I?"

"This might be a lot to ask," I began timidly, "but could you bring Derek with you?"

"Have mercy," she said, shuddering, her broad forehead splitting into creases.

"Alex doesn't look injured. I don't think she'll scare him. Maybe when he gets home from school—"

She scooted away from me as if I'd raised my fist to strike her. "How cruel you are."

"I know some people aren't comfortable in hospitals or rehab facilities, but children are resilient. It would mean a lot to Alex."

Dianna drew herself to her feet with effort. "You'd better leave."

"But why—"

She shook with anger. "Get out of my house."

"What did I say?"

"How dare you mock me."

"Honestly, I'm not—"

She sat back down, almost falling into the couch. "You don't know?"

I gestured helplessly. "What?"

She closed her eyes, reopened them, looked upward and took a trembling breath. "My boy passed almost two years ago."

I felt as if someone had sucked the air from my lungs. "Derek's dead?"

"He was electrocuted in a pond," Dianna Wallace said, swaying. "How am I supposed to take him on a visit anywhere?"

CHAPTER 7

Now I knew why Alex Madigen had thrown up at the mention of Derek Wallace's name.

I wondered how many more memories she'd buried, exhumed and reburied.

Sorry to say, I wouldn't find out on this day and not for lack of trying.

I drove from Dianna Wallace's apartment to Sinclair Rehabilitation Center, only delaying long enough to call Stacey Wilhite, but at the front desk, the receptionist shook her head when she noticed which resident I'd come to see.

"Alex isn't receiving visitors," she said before returning to the job at hand, attaching mailing labels to newsletters.

"She'll see me. I'm Kristin Ashe. Melissa, the other receptionist, knows me."

"Melissa's on vacation, and I'm following procedure."

"Is there a list of approved visitors? I must be on it." I read her nametag, "Holly."

She never looked up. "You're not."

"Could you call Alex in her room?"

"She asked not to be disturbed."

"This no-visitor request, is it coming from her or her family?"

"Federal privacy-protection laws prevent me from revealing information about the residents."

"Where's Kelly Nagle? She'll vouch for me."

"In a meeting."

"Where's your boss? Let me talk to her."

"In the same meeting," Holly said with a smug smile, which prompted me to march past her desk. She halted me with a jolly, "I wouldn't do that if I were you. If I have to call security, you'll be permanently banned."

I retreated, glaring at her. "Fine!"

"Sorry." She shrugged. "You shouldn't take it personally."

"How am I supposed to not take this personally?"

"Sometimes residents experience setbacks and don't feel up to receiving visitors. I'm sure Alex will come around in a few days, when she's feeling better."

Come around in a few days.

Alex Madigen had damn well better, or that would be the last of me coming around.

Over the next forty-eight hours, I rang up Alex repeatedly, never netting a return call, and by the forty-ninth hour of silence, I'd had enough.

On Wednesday, I drove to the rehab center, glanced in the front window, caught a glimpse of Holly in the sentinel position and kept driving, around to the side lot. I'd noticed on a previous visit that residents and staff used a door on the north side to access a smoking patio, and, contrary to posted regulations, they often left it propped open, even when no one was outside puffing.

Today was no exception, and I easily gained entrance to the building and located Alex in her room, centered on the bed, which had been stripped of all coverings. Wearing silk pajamas the color of red wine, she lay on her back, as if she'd been placed in a coffin, hands folded across her pelvis, ankles together.

"Did I do something to offend you?"

Alex rose slowly to a seated position and used the headboard as a backrest. "Kris, hello. No, why do you ask?"

"I've been trying to get in touch with you for two days, but it turns out I wasn't on your approved visitors list."

Her face looked drawn. "I wasn't feeling up to conversation."

"You could have come to the phone one of the thirty times I called and said that."

"I'm not comfortable on the phone. The pauses and silences disturb my sense of—"

"Alex!"

She gestured helplessly. "I can see you're upset, but I have good days and bad—"

I interrupted again, this time in a softer tone. "I'm on your side."

"No matter what kind of day?"

I sat at the table, resisting the urge to pound on it. "Regardless. Just come to the phone and say you can't talk."

She cast an apprehensive glance toward me. "I could do that? You wouldn't mind?"

"No, but if this is going to work, we have to keep a line of communication open."

"Is it working now?"

"I hope so. I have some news to share—"

"I do, as well," she cut in anxiously. "Last night, I had a dream inside a dream. In the dream, I'm sleeping, deep into a magical trance. Someone is touching me, making me full and throbbing. Her hand becomes my hand, kneading and teasing, thrusting and skimming. Inside my dream, I stir and touch myself, reaching inside my gown, between the cords and catheter. Arousing from the first dream, I feel that I'm dry, realize it was all a dream, and in the second dream, I begin to cry. When I awaken for good, I'm here, it's three o'clock in the morning and a nurse's aide is at my side."

I took a deep breath. "By open line of communication, I didn't necessarily mean I need to hear about your sexual dreams."

"Aren't they relevant?"

I rubbed my neck. "Maybe. How old are you in the dream?"

"I must be the age I am now? I'm thirty-seven, aren't I?"

I nodded. "Who is she, the woman in the first dream?"

"I don't know. In the dream, I never see her face, only the small of her back and a birthmark." Alex leaned forward. "You must find her for me."

"Are you kidding?" I kept my tone light. "Where am I supposed to start?"

Alex's eyes narrowed. "Begin by finding out if we ever met."

They think I can't remember, but I can.

I froze her in time, in the youth we left behind.

I conjured up memories of a teenage girl with perfect skin and a careless smile, and over the years, I couldn't stop thinking about her. No matter how hard I tried, I couldn't remove her from my mind.

One day, the new phone book arrived, and I looked up my own name and counted all the people with the same last name. Six in the Denver metro area. I looked up Stacey's name. The phone company had deleted her the year before, but she'd be pleased to know she was back. I started to close the book, but something compelled me to look up another name.

When I saw the letters and corresponding phone number, I felt as if my heart would explode.

According to the three-digit prefix, she lived in my neighborhood, tens of miles from where we'd met.

This was too close. How close? Her address was unlisted. I called information, but they refused to reveal the street. No one would tell me anything more than, "Withheld at customer's request."

A wave of panic captured me. Somehow, I'd always imagined that she'd left Colorado, on to bigger and better dreams, and the need to know where she lived took over my life.

Throughout that weekend, I called information, hoping to catch an operator off-guard. With no success by Monday morning, I was desper-

*ate enough to employ deceit. I called the customer service department
of the phone company and used her name. I claimed I hadn't received
last month's bill and needed to know the amount I owed. I had the
representative verify my address, and he reeled off numbers and the name
of a street.*

Panting, I lowered the phone to the cradle.

*She lived six blocks down and two blocks over from the home I shared
with Stacey.*

After almost twenty years, how dare she come this close to me?

"I'll know her if I see her," Alex said after an uncomfortable
pause.

"How?"

"I just will. I'll sense the connection. How could something in a
dream feel so real unless it happened to me? I hear the sound of water
running for a bath. I see slivers of sun on the bed. I just can't picture
her," she said, her frustration seeming to mount.

"It's not Stacey?"

"No. Of that, I'm certain."

"Okay." I made a point of pulling out my notebook and writing in it, more to demonstrate respect than as a reminder. "Back to
Stacey for a second."

Alex tore her attention away from the window, through which a
maintenance man could be seen mowing the lawn. "Yes?"

"I don't know how to tell you, but—"

"Derek's dead. That's why you're here."

"You remembered?"

"No, but Stacey told me on Monday. She wants me to fire you
because of a phone call you made to her. She didn't appreciate being
addressed in a rude manner."

I refrained from rolling my eyes. "When I asked about Derek,
Stacey was cooperative enough to give me his mother's name, address
and phone number but conveniently forgot to tell me that he died."

Alex looked at me impassively. "Stacey might not have known."

"Derek died almost two years ago, and Stacey attended his

memorial service. The two of you sat in the front row next to Dianna Wallace, his mother."

"I don't remember."

My tone became more heated. "But you'd think Stacey would, wouldn't you?"

"Yes, of course," Alex said, seeming jarred. "How did you find out he died?"

"I met with Dianna on Monday. She told me after I asked if she could bring Derek to see you when he came home from school."

Alex's face lost all color. "How did she—"

"In general, the meeting went well," I said brusquely, leaving out the part about Dianna's raw-throated cries.

"Did Dianna agree to see me? Will she come by?"

"She hasn't stopped in?" I said before recalling the ban on visitors.

"Not yet."

"Dianna said she'd come. I'm sure she will, but you need to tell the receptionist at the front desk to let her in."

"Yes. I will. Did Dianna like me? Could you tell?"

"She had nothing but good things to say. You were her rock after Derek died. You never left her side, often bringing her meals or staying with her overnight."

"How did he die?"

"On a camping trip."

She froze. "And?"

"You want the details?"

"I need them."

My voice remained even. "Dianna and Derek went on a camping trip with a group from their church. They were staying in the mountains outside of Granby."

"Yes . . ."

"Derek waded into a pond on a private golf course near the campground, probably to retrieve stray golf balls."

She swallowed hard. "Go on."

"A hot wire was strung in the water, from a plug in an outlet to a log."

"For what purpose?" Alex said mechanically.

"To ward off beavers."

"Derek touched the wire?"

I took a deep breath and nodded. "He became entangled in it. Other campers heard Derek's screams but couldn't do anything. The water made the electrical current stronger. His muscles contracted, and he couldn't move."

Alex lurched forward, almost hitting her head on her knees, which she'd bound together with her hands. Reflexively, I jumped up to assist, but she waved me off. "No one could save him?"

I backed away, returning to my seat. "They did everything they could, but they never revived him. Dianna made the decision to take him off life support."

She straightened up, in jerky motions. "Before I could see him one last time?"

"Yes."

Her teeth began to chatter. "Dianna didn't call me?"

"No, not until after Derek was pronounced dead."

"I wasn't permitted to visit him at the medical center before he died?"

"No, you weren't," I said, looking at her closely. "You remember Derek was transported to a medical center, not a hospital?"

Startled, she replied, "Yes."

"Medical personnel worked on his body for several hours, but it didn't make a difference. He died in the pond. You didn't miss anything."

"I missed him," she said simply.

"If it makes you feel any better, you were the first person Dianna called."

"What did I say?"

"Not much. You spoke for a few minutes and then hung up so that you could drive to Granby to be with her."

"When she told me Derek had died, did I cry?"

I said softly, "No."

"I didn't think so." Alex stared ahead blankly for a few moments, before adding, "I wonder what I did without him."

•••

They think I can't remember, but I can.

One day, and the day after and the next, I drove to her apartment building on Pearl Street, but I never left the car.

I simply watched.

In the early morning hours, I saw her leave for work. She came bounding out the door at six, while I sat slumped, downing cups of tea, willing alertness from languor. In the evenings, I held vigil for hours. Sometimes, she arrived home by four; other times I lingered until eight and still missed her.

What work did she do that yielded this flexibility? Did she stop somewhere between an office and home? Did she pursue a hobby or donate her time? Did she visit a lover? This last thought disheartened me immensely. I was in a committed relationship, yet I wanted her to be free, untouched and unhindered.

Eventually, I tired of the investment of hours to share seconds.

I needed more.

I decided I would follow her when she left her apartment, shadow her for an entire day. I would do what she did, go where she went, be what she was.

I would do this next Friday.

I understood that I was reaching beyond justification, but I couldn't stop.

For days that had stretched into weeks that had dissolved into months that had collapsed into years, my life had held no meaning.

This felt like my only chance.

CHAPTER 8

On the way back to the office, I reflected on Alex Madigen's latest appeal, to find a woman who may or may not exist and identify her from a birthmark in the small of her back.

No problem. As soon as I wrapped up that assignment, I'd skip to the moon.

I shook my head and muttered as I drove, only interrupting the perseveration long enough to whip into Good Times Burgers. I came away with a tray of cheeseburgers, fries and grasshopper shakes and arrived back at the office a few minutes ahead of Fran.

When I saw her park in front of the window, I breathed a sigh of relief at the sight of her purple Ford Ranger.

"You gave back the Lexus," I said by way of greeting when she came in and threw her fanny pack on the desk.

"Not without a fight." She plucked a fry from my hand. "Got us off the hook by agreeing to a date with Henny Carmichael. Me, not you. Don't have to thank me. Didn't mind taking one for the team."

"A date can't be much of a hardship. You've been slowing down lately."

"Ain't that the truth." Fran positioned one buttock on her desk and ran her fingers through her hair, returning most of the locks to a straight-up position. "Dating's never been easy. Back in the day, had to watch out for the lovelies who only wanted ass, gas or grass. Nowadays, in my age bracket, it's the nurse or the purse. Gotta be on guard. First dates are hard to come by, but I aim to remedy that."

I slid a tray of food across her desk. "You've slipped from three dates a week to two?"

She dropped into her chair. "More like one. Or none. Thanks for the grub. What do I owe you?"

"Nothing. You bought last time."

"That I did." She used a straw to stir whipped cream from the top of the drink into the green shake, sloshing liquid over the side of the cup. I tossed her a napkin, but she cleaned up the spill with her index finger and lips. "Gotta step up my game. Usual methods aren't producing enough leads. Online's at a crawl. Profile must have gone stale. Grocery store, only so many times you can hang out in the produce section before the manager threatens to call the police. Four or five per week, max, case you're wondering."

I smiled. "I wasn't."

Fran unwrapped her cheeseburger, removed the bun and ate the two pickles. "Speed dating's out. Recycling through the same crowd."

"Book club?"

She licked mustard from her fingers. "Booted me out for not reading the books. Thought the point was socializing, not literary enrichment. Before you ask about bowling, too many gutter balls. Couldn't break the C-mark with any regularity. Nothing to be ashamed about. Not everyone's born with command of the hardwoods."

"Gay Bingo?"

"Had to give up that, too. Couldn't work out a satisfactory schedule with Ruth. Bumped into the ex one too many times and was politely asked to leave."

"That's not fair. You have as much right—"

"Spilled coffee. In her lap. Don't know how it happened." Fran reassembled her cheeseburger and took a massive bite, swallowing after three chomps. "Mulling over talk radio. That's my latest, greatest idea."

"How can you meet women through talk radio?"

Fran prepared to bite into four fries at once. "Host my own show."

I shot her a look. "At the age of sixty-seven, you intend to break into broadcasting?"

"Why not? Saw an ad in *Out Front* for a lesbian-oriented forum. One-hour spot on Thursdays. Maybe the producers'll love the whole ex-nun thing, and don't worry, I won't get a big head. Not even when I become a star, and groupies start hanging around."

"You're supposed to be working full-time," I said pointedly.

"Not a problem." She pointed both thumbs at her chest. "All caught up. Wrapped up my old lady case. Turned the caregiver over to the authorities. Got the deed transferred back in Grandma's name. Ran background checks on the new live-in. All's well that ends well."

I took a sip from my shake, regretting that I hadn't supersized it. "What about researching Alex Madigen's accident?"

She wiped ketchup from her cheek, spreading it to her chin. "Meeting Friday with the trooper who processed the scene. Got that handled."

"And the marketing plans for the business? What happened to those?"

She waved at me with her burger. "Still attending chamber meetings and expanding the circle of influence. Don't you worry. Got promo covered, full calendar of activities. Think of radio as my new hobby."

"Your hobbies are more time-consuming than most people's jobs. Fantasy football, snowboarding, golf. Now this!"

"Everything's under control," Fran said tranquilly. "You want to hear about my babe-bagging opportunity or not?"

I replied with no enthusiasm, "Sure."

She brightened. "Have an interview next Monday. Look over my list of topics, would you?" She reached under her blotter and handed me a scrap of paper. "Which's your favorite?"

I scanned the short list. "'Lesbian bed death—what to do.'"

She raised an eyebrow. "Any particular reason?"

"Because it applies to more women than 'Vegans living with meat lovers—what's the beef?' You need to come up with more than two topics if you really want the job."

"Counting on you to add to the list," she said with a cajoling grin.

"Commitment ceremonies—what to wear."

"Good, good," she said, fumbling to get the cap off her pen.

"Company picnics—should girlfriends go?"

Fran nodded approval. "Timely, with barbeque season in full swing. I like how you think. Hold on a sec, though. Bed death jogged my memory. Did our decoy target call you back?"

I nodded. "Monday afternoon. I left a note on your desk."

She shuffled through mounds of papers. "Got it. Appointment with Linda Palizzi, Thursday at lunchtime. Yikes, that's tomorrow! How'd the initial contact go? Spill!"

"There's nothing to tell. She described the house for rent in Bonnie Brae, and we agreed to meet there during her lunch hour."

"No big deal, right?"

I eyed her warily. "So far."

"Told you." She leaned across the space between our desks and smacked me on the arm. "You're a natural, kid. This could be big. Bigger than big. Gargantuan. We'll put Test-A-Mate franchises in every city. Am I good, or what?" She paused to pat herself on the back. "Everything's unfolding according to plan. Yes, it is."

Unfolding according to plan.

Easy for Fran Green to say when she didn't have to expose potential cheaters.

What about me, the one doing all the work? How did I feel?

Truthfully?

I couldn't shake a sense of dread.

• • •

Dread followed me home that night, only lifting temporarily when Destiny called from San Francisco. I laughed at her recap of thirty lesbians spending sixty collective hours to construct a solitary sentence on domestic partnerships and shared with her Fran's broadcasting ambitions.

We spent twenty minutes chatting, and when I hung up, I couldn't help but focus on the days to go before Destiny would rejoin me, rather than on the ones that had passed since she left.

I hated coming home to an empty house and eating alone, and I hated sleeping alone.

Destiny's presence helped alleviate my chronic insomnia, and without it, more often than not, I was doomed to eight or ten hours of restlessness, a pattern I repeated on this Wednesday evening.

To get a headstart on the process, I went to bed early, but as the night crept into its darkest hours, I felt overwhelmed by what lay ahead.

Sometime after sunrise, I would have to return to Alex Madigen's room at Sinclair and attempt to extract more information about a mysterious woman who, in all likelihood, lived only in Alex's fantasies. And before sunset, I would have to meet Linda Palizzi at her rental house in Bonnie Brae and pretend I was a prospective tenant, all the while attempting to record flirting or inappropriate behavior, information I would pass on to her life partner, Roxanne Herbert.

Given the circumstances of the Thursday to come, it made sense that I couldn't sleep.

I didn't want to wake up.

My deepest periods of slumber came between six and nine in the morning, which meant I had to skip a thirty-minute workout in the basement, and I yawned all the way to Sinclair, almost missing the entrance to the grounds.

Skidding through a turn, I continued down the windy lane at a crawl. Formerly the site of a girl's boarding school, the campus had been transformed into a healthcare hub. Four modern stucco buildings housed a medical center, nursing home, assisted living facility and Sinclair, and they were sprinkled among turn-of-the-century brick structures that served as administrative offices. Ten acres of peaceful surroundings included walking paths and flower beds, elms and silver maples and benches and picnic tables.

I parked in front of Sinclair and at the front desk exchanged pleasantries with Melissa, the receptionist who had returned from a Vegas vacation, and ignored Holly, the substitute who lurked in the background. From there, I dropped by the activities room and found a resident playing the piano, one agonizing note at a time, but no sign of Alex.

After a brief debate over what to do next, I headed to the staff wing to track down Kelly Nagle, to thank her for referring Alex's case to me. I reached her office and was poised to knock on the partially open door when I realized she was in a meeting with Stacey Wilhite.

Both women were seated, Kelly behind her desk and Stacey off to the side of the room with her back to the door. Neither noticed my arrival or my retreat at the first snatch of conversation.

What would Fran Green do?

That was easy. Stay and eavesdrop, and who was I to contradict the morals of an ex-nun? I slinked forward and leaned against the wall.

"Alex isn't ready to come home," I heard Stacey say.

"She told you that?" Kelly replied.

"No, but I know. She has trouble with simple tasks and won't pay attention. She can't make decisions and doesn't want to drive. She's having problems with balance. And her mood swings . . ." Stacey's voice trailed off.

Kelly said gently, "I understand your apprehension, but the change won't be as drastic as you might imagine. Alex will come to Sinclair five days a week for physical and occupational therapy."

"I'd prefer she live here for a few more months."

"No offense, but that's not up to you. At this point, delaying Alex's release would only serve to stunt her."

"What if she fails?"

"She deserves the chance to try. We've arranged for transportation and meals. She'll have a nurse on call twenty-four hours a day. Between therapy and support groups, she'll be at Sinclair twenty or thirty hours per week."

"She can't live with me indefinitely."

"I don't believe that's her intent. The goal is to decrease her reliance on you, to push for as much self-sufficiency as possible. Have you talked to her about any of this?"

"Every time I try, she pretends she's in pain or can't remember."

"I doubt she's pretending. Most of our patients fake abilities, not disabilities."

"When will Alex be normal?"

"There is no normal."

"You know what I mean."

"I'm afraid I don't."

Stacey let out an exasperated sigh. "She doesn't even realize she's changed."

"Every brain injury is different. Recovery varies from patient to patient, and healing takes time. I wish we could speed up the process, but we can't. Individuals recover at their own pace."

"When will she be back to being herself?"

"This *is* herself. The physical, emotional, behavioral and cognitive challenges have altered Alex's life."

"You don't understand."

"I might. I've worked in this field for a number of years. Alex doesn't look different, so you might assume she's fine, but more often than not, it feels to you as if you're having a relationship with a stranger. When you do catch glimpses of who she was, they make you wish for more. Is that fairly accurate?"

"Yes." There was a long silence, and I strained to hear the continuation. "She used to be beautiful and self-reliant, calm and reserved. She never expressed anger. She had a sharp memory and was extremely intelligent."

Kelly spoke. "Now she's easily frustrated, slow to make connections, less concerned with her appearance. She doesn't have the resilience to rebound from daily setbacks. She has chronic pain syndrome, which can cause day-to-day personality shifts. Her self-image has suffered. I understand how you feel, but Alex is ready for the next step. Are you?"

Stacey sniffled. "What am I supposed to do the nights I'm on call?"

"You're a social worker, correct?"

"Yes. I work for the Denver Coroner's Office."

"I'm sure something could be arranged, but it sounds to me as if you've made up your mind. Perhaps we should be making alternate plans for Alex's release."

"When will Alex recover her long-term memory? Do you know that?"

"It's hard to say. The inability to remember is one of the symptoms commonly associated with Alex's type of injury. The process of retrieving old memories and forming and retaining new ones is ongoing."

"How much does she remember?"

"That's impossible to tell. There's a common misconception about memory, that it acts as a storage system from which we can retrieve information intact. Research has shown, however, that capturing memory is more of a reconstruction process. We assemble pieces, based on experiences and perceptions, followed by fact-checking, if you will. Alex may be missing, at least for the moment, the ability to separate fact from fiction and the skills required to place particular happenings in order."

"I'm sure Alex knows more than she's admitting."

"Possibly, but that's not uncommon. Certain memories might confuse or frighten her. They could be coming in jumbled or, worse, vividly enough to seem as if they're happening in real time. Protective mechanisms might prevent Alex from remembering specific events or emotions."

"Ever?"

"Ever."

"Lucky her," Stacey said sullenly.

"Pardon?"

"Why do I have to remember?"

"I assume in your line of work, you help people cope with bad news?"

"I would hope so. I'm called to the scenes of accidents, murders and suicides."

"Do you enjoy what you do?"

"It fulfills me."

"Always sudden deaths?" Kelly asked.

"Typically."

"Did your training help prepare you when you first heard about Alex's accident?"

"No."

"Why?"

After a long pause, Stacey said, "Because she didn't die."

Reflexively, I peeked in the office and stifled an expletive.

In the courtyard, a few feet beyond the open screen door, out of Kelly's and Stacey's view, I saw a figure doubled over, as if struggling for breath.

When Alex Madigen straightened up, our eyes locked.

CHAPTER 9

I found Alex in her room, in the center of the bed, knees pressed against her chest, arms tightly wound, head down. I pulled up a chair and sat next to her. "Are you okay?"

"I feel a little lightheaded," she mumbled.

"How much did you hear?"

"Enough."

"I'm sorry."

She took a deep breath, cocked her head and glanced at me out of the corner of her eye. "It's better that I know, isn't it?"

I nodded. "Do you remember what Stacey wants to forget?"

"Yes."

They think I can't remember, but I can.
I could hardly wait.
Soon I would be spending twenty-four hours with her, and I planned

the day with care, scheduling it for a time when Stacey was attending a bereavement workshop in Dallas.

I rid my calendar of all obligations and filled the car with food, water and a makeshift bedpan. I loaded my iPod and packed a handful of newspapers, magazines and books. I arranged a change of clothes and disguises and tucked maps of Denver and Colorado in the glove compartment.

On the appointed day, I was ready for anything when we began before dawn, precisely at six.

She came out of her apartment building, bundled against the cold. An overcoat stretched to the tops of stylish, mid-calf, black boots, and a scarf was wrapped around her neck, chin and nose, almost reaching to the brim of her snowcap. She strode toward her Volvo in the south lot and scraped the front window, removing a layer of bumpy ice, before driving off.

Light snow was falling, but the roads we traveled had been cleared, and in the dark commute, I kept my distance. When she pulled up in front of a warehouse in an industrial section of northwest Denver, I drove past without hesitation.

Minutes later, I was back, reading a placard that listed four businesses: performance arts studio, kitchen remodeling center, caterer and prosthetics designer. Which one of these enterprises did she work for or own?

While she was inside the building, I had hours to contemplate her life's work. Was she a dancer, a decorator, a chef or a body-parts builder? I couldn't begin to know. The last time we'd spoken, she was enamored with soccer and photography.

Our day together passed slowly, and shortly after seven, we were on the move again. When it was apparent that our route was a reversal of the morning's drive, I took side streets and shortcuts and arrived at her apartment before she did. A bitter wind hurried her into the entryway, and she grabbed mail and scurried through the inside door.

Within seconds, I saw lights brighten her corner unit, and I assumed she was in for the night, a night I was prepared to spend with her.

At ten o'clock, however, she proved me wrong by exiting the building.

• • •

My voice rose as I repeated, "What do you remember?"

"A feeling that my life was out of control," Alex replied, lifting her head as if awakened. "I was possessed by something or someone. I remember driving around, following her."

"Was it Stacey? Was she having an affair?"

"I don't know."

"The woman in your dreams, is that who you were following?"

"I can't say."

I softened my tone. "Did you complete the sketch of the birthmark?"

She shook her head and whispered, "I couldn't. Dianna Wallace came by yesterday, after you left."

"How did it go? Did you recognize her?"

Alex sat up straight and ran a hand across the top of her head. "Thankfully, yes, but my appearance seemed to give her pause. She commented on my hair, or lack thereof."

"What did you talk about?"

"Derek. She brought me a check."

"For what?"

"A refund. She told me Derek used to help me write jingles. He came to a studio in the house I shared with Stacey. Is it still there?"

"The studio? No, Stacey moved," I reminded her.

"When?"

"The week before your accident."

Her brow wrinkled. "Where was I meant to live?"

"You bought a condo in Cherry Creek but hadn't moved into it."

"Do I still own it?"

"Yes."

She blinked rapidly. "What were we discussing?"

"Derek and the jingles. Do you remember working with him?"

"Only because of what Dianna told me." Alex rubbed her eyes, which were red and puffy. "Not independently."

I concealed my disappointment. "Why does Dianna want to give you money?"

"For my care. She and I had set up a fund in Derek's name, and I made royalty deposits for his college education—" Her voice caught. "The money doesn't belong to me. Could she use it?"

"Probably, but she might be too proud to accept it."

"I don't need it. I have insurance to pay my medical bills, and money still comes in from the jingles I wrote. A lot of it, apparently. I don't want Derek's money. What do you think I should do?"

I thought for a moment. "You could set up a scholarship in his name."

"Perhaps," she said, nodding. "Dianna brought in a picture of us, of him and me in a paddleboat at City Park."

"Where is it? Did she leave it?"

"In the drawer, but please don't remove it. I don't want to cry again."

I took my hand off the nightstand and leaned back. "Do you remember the day the photo was taken?"

"Not specifically, but it reminds me of his spirit, which makes me feel how much I missed him when he died."

"You remember that?"

She nodded. "I remember driving into the mountains to bring him home."

"From Granby," I said, almost under my breath.

"I tried to hold myself in but somehow fell out. No one understood my loss. Especially not Stacey."

I touched her hand, to still the shaking. "This can't be easy."

"This time," Alex said, withdrawing from my grasp, "I'll go through it, not around it."

"Grief?"

Her shoulders slumped. "Love."

"Are you sure you want to continue with what we're doing?"

"I'm prepared for the next step, if that's what you're asking."

"Do you know what the next step is, aside from gathering details about your crash and finding the woman with the birthmark?"

"The chorus." Her voice quivered. "Something happened to me at the last concert I played."

"Which was when?"

"I wrote it down," she said, reaching for a leather-bound book on the nightstand. "I asked my mother and made a note. The Colorado Lesbian Chorus. March second. Not this past March, but the one before."

"Was your mother at the concert?"

She shook her head. "She felt it was beneath me."

"Do you remember the performance?"

"Not the music as much as a connection."

"To the audience?"

She drew in a breath. "Yes. Of one."

"Was Stacey there?"

"I don't think so. I receive flashes of that night, but no reminders of her."

"Flashes?"

"From all sides. I need to know about the light in the darkness. I need to know which was which."

They think I can't remember, but I can.

I followed her in the dark to Oblivion.

I'd never stepped foot inside the city's hottest lesbian nightclub, but I'd read enough reviews to piece together hip dance music, strobe lights and big-screen televisions flashing lesbian porn. I couldn't help but ponder how many times she'd been in Oblivion. Did she meet friends or come alone? Did she cruise or wait to be cruised? Did she smoke, drink or do drugs?

She maneuvered her car into a slot between the alley and the building and walked toward the front door. I circled the parking lot until a space opened—one with a view of the entrance—and I backed in and waited.

I wore three layers of socks, two pairs of gloves and a heavy coat, yet I shook as I watched women come and go. Goths and button-downs, GenYs and boomers, singles and couples—they all seemed playful and happy.

The longer she stayed inside, the more agitated I became.

My drumming of fingers became a pounding of fists, and the light buzz in my head converted to a relentless hammering. I drank from a thermos and rubbed my hands and eyes. I yawned repeatedly and stretched my upper body, and at the conclusion of one long stretch, my eyes bulged, then I frowned, then I felt a crazed smile cross my face.

My mind had taken an alarming turn as I began to wonder . . . What could it hurt to go into the bar and look for her, to pretend to bump into her, to casually touch her arm?

I'd come this far, crossing all manner of boundaries. What could it hurt?

I pushed open the car door and placed my foot on the ground, moving slowly to determine if my cramped leg would bear weight. Biting back a groan from the pain in my left knee, I stood upright and saw that she was coming toward me, with less than a hundred feet separating us.

I had no time to run or crouch and nowhere to hide, but she was absorbed in another woman and passed without noticing me. Their bodies merged to form one silhouette, and their high-pitched laughter drowned out my crushed cry.

They clambered into a small pickup, which I followed.

"What could it hurt?" I screamed.

I was determined to fulfill my twenty-four hour commitment, to spend the beginning, middle and end of a day with her, but I felt shattered.

They returned to her apartment, and I spent the rest of the night outside in the cold.

Through half-closed eyes, I watched the digital clock on the dashboard, and when at last it released the numbers six, zero, zero, I moved my seat to an upright position and started the engine.

Pulling away from the curb, I drove a few car lengths before ramming into the small pickup.

With a faint smile, I reversed and drove away.

Alex Madigen's words continued to ring through my head an hour later, despite my best attempts to focus on Linda Palizzi, Roxanne Herbert's life partner.

Which was which? The light in the darkness.

On the one hand, I was trying to save a life, and on the other, I was preparing to ruin one.

I'd rushed home from Sinclair to try on at least sixteen different outfits before selecting a pale yellow silk blouse, brown moleskin pants, an Italian leather belt and low-heeled slides. For jewelry, I'd gone light—simple post earrings in tortoise and a matching cuff watch with steel dial. Superb choices, I thought, except that I now stood in front of 1042 South Columbine Street, tapestry jacket draped over my arm, wondering whether I should have worn something more alluring.

Linda Palizzi and I had walked through the rental house together, twice, and when she hadn't said or done anything inappropriate, my anxiety had intensified.

She'd arrived at our appointment a few minutes late, dressed in classic-tailored twill pants, a white oxford shirt with mother-of-pearl buttons and olive rubber-sole loafers. She looked fit, but I didn't detect enough musculature to back up any claim of ten hours per week at the gym. She had short, natural-blond hair, styled with a dab of gel, and a husky voice and infectious laugh, both of which I'd caught on tape, thanks to the microcassette recorder in my distressed leather purse.

As Linda and I lingered on the sidewalk, she said conversationally, "Are you interested?"

"In the house? I am, but it would be a big change."

"Where do you live?"

"Downtown, on the eleventh floor of Brooks Towers. I have a spectacular view of the mountains and lights of the city," I said, laying the groundwork for my ultimate rejection of the property.

Linda looked at me curiously. "Why do you want to move?"

"I miss having a yard. I'd love to grow vegetables and herbs."

She leaned in and said confidentially, "There's a fertile spot by the garage."

I nodded. "I saw that, but I'd miss my swimming pool and workout room."

"Are you out much?"

"Out?"

"Out and about?" she said, deep dimples emerging with her smile. "I don't know if you're familiar with this area, but from here, you can walk to Washington Park, Cherry Creek Mall and Old South Gaylord."

"That's convenient."

"Did you grow up in the Denver area?"

"I did. In Centennial, off Arapahoe Road," I answered candidly. Why lie when it didn't matter? "How about you?"

"Minneapolis."

"You're a long way from home."

"I moved here after college, with my . . . friend. Are you in a relationship? I'd put a second name on the lease if you are. Or leave it off, whichever you prefer."

I cleared my throat. "Er, no. I'm not."

"Are you leaning toward taking the house?"

"A slight tilt," I said, allowing a half-smile. "The rent's a little steep. I'm paying twelve hundred now."

"That is a jump."

Linda had quoted eighteen hundred dollars for the nine hundred-square-foot, red-brick Tudor. The interior was dated but clean, and the house was situated on a large lot with mature landscaping. The layout consisted of two bedrooms and a full bath upstairs, with an extra bedroom and three-quarters bath in the basement. Thousands of similar Tudors were sprinkled around the metro area—some in better shape, some in worse—but few came on the market as rentals, almost none in Bonnie Brae. At least that's how Linda had positioned the property.

"It's worth every cent, but I have to decide what I can afford."

"You could get a roommate to help offset expenses."

"I'm past that," I said lightly. "No roommates. Not unless they're sleeping in my bed."

Linda studied me with an air of quiet amusement. "Is there anything I can do to persuade you?"

"No. I love the house and block. I just need time."

"Don't wait too long. I have two more sets of people coming by this week."

"I'll do my best." I punched the remote to unlock my Honda. "I'd better get going. It was nice meeting you."

She leaned against the front panel of my car and ran a hand through her hair. "Likewise. I hope I'll see you again."

"You might."

"Call me if you have any questions."

My mouth felt dry. "I will."

She lowered her voice, almost to a whisper. "Or need anything."

We shook hands, and I climbed in and started the car engine. "Okay."

"Thanks for coming." Linda gently pushed the door shut and tapped a farewell on the window as I drove away.

When I came to the four-way stop at the end of the block and glanced in the rearview mirror, I could see her standing on the sidewalk, staring my way. I looked at my watch in disbelief. How could only twenty minutes have passed since I'd parked in front of the house? It felt as if I'd put in a ten-hour shift, a notion confirmed by the armpit stains on my blouse.

Damn that Fran Green for talking me in to decoy work.

Never again.

I spent the rest of Thursday afternoon subjected to Fran's ribbing for my failure to elicit anything incriminating from Linda Palizzi. She joked that I'd lost my "mojo." She nitpicked the tape to pieces, pointing out every opportunity I'd missed to "go in for the kill." She went on about my laxity in not loosening one more button on my shirt.

While I found none of this funny or supportive, I really didn't appreciate the fact that she refused to accept my resignation. She insisted I bring the Herbert-Palizzi case to a conclusion before rushing to judgment about our Test-A-Mate business.

Yeah, yeah, yeah.

I copied the tape for Roxanne Herbert, left a message on her cell phone and fled the office in order to put the whole mess out of my mind.

On Friday, when Fran and I met again, we avoided discussion of decoying only because she had more important news to share, information she'd gathered from the trooper who had processed Alex Madigen's accident scene.

Saturday afternoon, Fran and I delivered the findings to Alex in a meeting that was awkward, to say the least, but it wasn't until Monday morning that I discovered the full extent of the consequences.

CHAPTER 10

"I don't want her coming back," Alex said to me at the start of the workweek. I'd found her in the activities room, seated at the piano but not playing.

I retrieved a folding chair and scooted next to her, and the closer I came, the more her appearance alarmed me. She looked drawn and pale, and her eyes were almost swollen shut.

"Could you repeat that?" I said, not sure I'd heard correctly over the clamor of five residents who had gathered around a nearby table.

"I don't want her coming here."

"Who? Stacey? Your mother? Dianna?"

She tossed back her head. "Your associate."

I gulped. "Fran Green? Why?"

"She distracts me. I want to focus on you."

"Me?" I said, sounding like I had a bubble in my throat.

"Only you. Too much stimulation makes everything blurry."

"Fran can be stimulating," I conceded with a smile. "Still, I thought it would be easier if she explained the details of the accident, rather than having me relay them. I know the information was upsetting, but you asked for the truth."

"She doesn't understand me."

"She just met you."

"Because of my brain injury, I have increased sensitivity to lights, sounds and distractions. I can only do one thing at a time, and I tire easily. She made me feel tired."

I smiled again. "Fran has that effect on me, too."

"Never bring her again and don't let her work on my case. I don't want her to know anything about me. Do you hear me?" Alex shouted over the din.

"Yes," I said distractedly, already feeling anxious about the conversation with Fran.

They think I can't remember, but I can.

My excuses had piled up beyond any reasonable allotment.

Stacey viewed me with suspicion, if at all, and my mundane life seemed a lifetime ago, a now appealing but perhaps unreachable goal. For months, I'd planned activities around her schedule, controlled by whims at which I could only guess. My neck was permanently stiff from idle hours in the car, and I'd gained eight pounds from fortifying my interest with junk food.

On that day, however, I was determined to move to the next level, to get closer to her.

I held a bouquet of yellow roses and pressed buttons for different apartments, hoping to persuade someone to let me into the building.

An elderly woman answered on my fourth attempt. "Yes?"

"Flower delivery."

"What a surprise! I'm on the first floor, third door on the left."

With a buzz, I gained access and delivered the flowers before moving to the stairwell in the front of the building. On the landing between the second and third floor, through a large glass window, I had a clear view of the street.

I alternated between sitting and standing, and while I waited, I contemplated the work she'd chosen. On the Internet, I'd learned more about her career. Astonishingly, she was the prosthetics designer. According to her Web site, she could make eyes with red silk thread to imitate blood vessels. To noses and ears, she added blemishes of sunspots, blotches, freckles and skin discoloration. She made breasts, as well. In fact, the Cancer Foundation had presented an award to her five years earlier, one she'd accepted only after crediting breast cancer survivors with "the true heroism."

I'd been digesting this news about her professional calling for weeks, and it continued to prickle. How could she, someone with an utter lack of vanity, toil for hours in pursuit of physical perfection? Every shirt she used to own held traces of food stains, and days would pass before she washed her hair, as if social necessities only clung to other people.

I would have believed she ran a performance arts studio, kitchen remodeling center or catering business, but lashes, lids and sockets? Fingers and toes? Made for victims of accidents, injuries and illnesses? She might have replaced losses from burned flesh, torn body parts and surgical removals, but how could she deal with the finer points of art without addressing the attached emotions?

Who did she think she was?

How dare she reconstruct physical form and expect it to erase grief.

Her audacity stirred me to a degree that I almost missed her homecoming. Deep in thought, I overlooked her entrance into the building and only become aware of her presence when voices surged in the stairwell. The haunting, deep timbre of hers seduced me again, as if no time had passed. In me, the sound triggered a primal release, and I stumbled toward the next landing, narrowly avoiding confrontation.

"If you want to give me a key to your apartment, Leah, fine. But I won't use it, and I won't give you a key to this place," she said.

"Why? What's scaring you?"

"I don't want to exchange keys. Can't we leave it at that?"

As their voices faded and a door slammed, I comprehended for the first time the span of my actions, a realization that struck me like a well-placed blow. I pressed against my temples to mute the pounding, but nothing could stem the rising tide of nausea.

I ran toward the back of the building and down the stairs, barely making it out the back door in time. Vomit flew across the length of the Dumpster, and chills began, rendering me helpless with uncontrollable shaking.

This was no way to live.

I knew I was sick, but from the past or the present?

I wasn't sure what kind of life I could design, but it couldn't include her.

Positively, this was the last time I would seek her out.

"You can't fire me. Nice try, but no can do," Fran said thirty minutes later when I returned to the office. She raked her desktop Zen garden in a frenzy. "Last I checked, papers we signed in January split the business down the middle."

"I'm not trying to fire you," I said for the second time as I brushed sand from my leg. "I'm asking you to step aside on one case."

"Never made that request before."

"I've never had to. This is the first time a client's complained."

"A brain-addled one." Fran pointed the pen-sized rake at me. "No coincidence there. Why you pinning this one on me, skipper? Who asked me along as first mate, begged me to work a Saturday?"

"I made a mistake," I said wearily. "I thought it would be easier if Alex heard the reconstruction information from you directly. Obviously I was wrong."

Fran scoffed and rolled back her head. "She's playing you like a fiddle."

"Wouldn't piano be the more apt metaphor?"

"You catch my meaning. That woman couldn't take her eyes off you. Not for a second."

"You're imagining things."

"How many cases we worked together?"

"Twenty-six. At least that's the number you brought up at our last shareholder's meeting."

"How many times you kicked me to the curb?"

"None, but—"

"My point's made." Fran leaned back in her chair and clasped her hands behind her head.

"This case is different."

"How so?"

"I told you. The client requested it."

Fran shot forward and almost fell onto her desk. "Look me in the eye, straight on. Left eye, not the wandering one. There you go. Now tell me what you feel for this Alex Madigen."

I didn't hesitate. "Sympathy."

"Nothing more?"

"Of course not. Did it ever occur to you that I might be playing her?"

"Destiny know about this?"

"This is business!" I said between clenched teeth. "I've seen Destiny turn it on to get a donation."

"Betcha she never played footsie with a brain-injured woman to win her over."

"Alex doesn't trust anyone and probably never has. To earn her trust, I'm letting her be herself, whoever that self is. Maybe you should have tried the same."

Fran shrugged. "Not my fault she didn't like what I had to say."

"It was your delivery!"

"Too technical?"

I let out a grunt. "When you started covering the time-distance studies, you lost me."

"A woman crosses her legs, aims the big toe at someone, dead giveaway of interest. Her gam was locked on you like a rifle. Don't try to deny it."

"What were you thinking with those vector sum analyses?"

"Miss Memory Loss had no trouble mirroring the tone and speed of your voice."

"Alex is learning speech patterns. Algorithms of driver-related risk factors," I said accusingly. "Didn't you see our eyes glazing over?"

"Couldn't tell with her. Never looked at me. Not once."

"That lecture on advances in reconstruction software and calculations of momentum? Come on!"

"Thought the air speed of the vehicle after it careened off the pile was relevant."

"You were so busy praising the first responders, you forgot you were talking to the victim."

"Did no such thing," Fran said tartly. "When you left to go to the bathroom, soon as you came back, she squared herself, lifted her shoulders. That tell you anything?"

"G-forces in occupant kinematics? Who's ever heard of that word?"

"Might want to step it down a notch from hysterical."

"Please! Trying to impress us with peak loads. 'Force equals mass times acceleration.' What the hell were you doing?"

Fran shook her head slowly. "You tell me."

I suddenly felt dejected. "You acted like this was research for a science project. How can you close down like that when the woman whose body was ravaged is sitting right in front of you? We didn't need a lesson in calculus and physics."

"Heck you didn't. Neither one of you mules wanted to believe the expert."

I could barely speak. "*Mules?*"

"Stubborn as. You send me off to interview a Colorado Highway Patrol investigator. Here's what she tells me. Closed down the inter-state for five hours to conduct the investigation. Photographed and videotaped the scene. Took measurements of debris and skid marks. Made sketches and perspective grids and turned those into scale drawings. Evaluated the roadway and weather conditions. Factored in night visibility limitations. Collected statements from three cred-ible witnesses. Analyzed vehicle dynamics and damage. Know what our expert concluded?"

"I heard it the first time. In Alex's room, when she was wincing in pain."

"You want accident reconstruction for dummies? Why didn't you say so? No evidence of lane change, swerving, braking, steering avoidance or vehicle malfunction. Need it simpler? Here goes." Fran clenched her teeth. "On the clear, dry night of August sixteenth, at approximately eleven o'clock, Alex Madigen drove her Toyota

Camry into a concrete pile at the Quincy overpass on Interstate Twenty-Five. Estimated speed, ninety-one miles per hour. Car went airborne. She flew out of it. That simple enough for you?"

"I got it!"

"No drugs or alcohol in her system. Seems I'm the only one who wants to accept the truth, the only one in this office not acting like a lap dog."

"How's the truth going to help Alex's healing process? How does she benefit from you rubbing it in that she tried to kill herself but didn't succeed?"

"Shame my efforts aren't appreciated."

"You didn't have to sound like a state trooper." I mimicked Fran's deeper voice. "Proximate cause of accident was driver error."

Fran's lips tightened. "You object to my style, bench me."

"I just did."

"Fine."

"Fine!" I took a deep breath. "Couldn't you at least have given Alex hope?"

"Didn't know that's the business we're in."

"Accidents occur in milliseconds of time. Couldn't you have said that?"

"Says *Investigator* on my business card, not *Nursemaid*."

"Someone's life is at stake. Don't you get it?"

She stood, leaned across my desk and snapped her fingers in my face. "Yours or hers?"

"Where are you going?"

"Interview for my talk show," Fran said, heading toward the door. "We're through here."

We were not through.

Not even close.

For the next few hours, I relived our argument, replaying remarks I'd made, replacing them with better barbs, but eventually I acknowledged that Fran might have been accurate on a few points. When I couldn't reach her on her cell, I decided instead to set matters straight with Alex Madigen.

I drove back to the rehab center, intent on explaining that I was in charge of her case and would decide when and how to use Fran Green.

If Alex didn't agree, she could fire me.

Unfortunately, I couldn't deliver my speech, because when I came upon her she was on the verge of tears. Seated at the round table in her room, she was across from a woman who seemed equally stressed, and I watched for a moment as they studied an album.

"That's the Empire State building in New York. Your father took this picture the first weekend we came for a lesson with Gideon Conlon."

"How old was I?" Alex asked.

"You had just turned ten."

"Why were we in New York?"

"There were no world-class pianists in Colorado. We had to look elsewhere to nurture your talent."

"Is this a picture of me when I played with a chorus?"

"I've told you before, you didn't play with a chorus until a few years ago. I didn't approve of your participation and neither did Stacey."

Alex scowled, closed her eyes and took a deep breath.

They think I can't remember, but I can.

Stacey didn't trust me.

She never had.

Was my self-distrust the cause of this or the result?

Regardless, I'd isolated myself over the years until our togetherness had driven me apart. I'd caved in, until I was almost unable to reach out.

One day, however, in a brief window of impulse, I chose to act deliberately. I e-mailed the conductor of the Colorado Lesbian Chorus to offer my musical services. She called within an hour of the query and invited me to lunch the next day, an audition without music, although she had the grace not to frame it as such.

To Stacey, I said nothing of the meeting, and driving to the suburban steakhouse, I felt as if I were cheating on her, a reaction that intensified when the conductor and I clicked instantly. We traded verbal résumés and industry horror stories, and by dessert, I had committed to an engagement with the chorus.

Without informing Stacey.

A fact she pointed out to me over laundry later that night. "I thought you never wanted to play the piano again."

I methodically creased underwear and bras, and Stacey paired socks. "I want to try."

"You said you were done with music forever."

"I changed my mind."

"Why the Colorado Lesbian Chorus? Why didn't you contact the Denver Philharmonic or your former agent?"

"The chorus is an amateur group. They'll be made no better or worse by my accompaniment."

"Won't their skill level frustrate you?"

"Probably."

"How much time will this take from us?"

"Rehearsals once a week, two or three concerts per year and four weekend retreats."

"I hope they don't practice on Wednesday nights."

"We do," I said, my first expression of belonging.

"But I'm on call Tuesdays and Thursdays, and I have my grief group on Mondays."

"I know."

Stacey took a sheet out of the dryer and handed one end to me. In four efficient motions, we shook out the wrinkles and folded it with precision. After we repeated the task, I stood awkwardly as she continued to fold shirts and pants.

"Where do they go on retreats?" she asked.

"I have no idea."

"What's the point?"

"Coming together as a group, I would imagine."

"Aren't weekly rehearsals enough?"

"Evidently not."

"Would you share a room with other women?"

"*I assume so.*"

"*Are most of the women in the chorus single or in partnerships?*"

"*The exact percentage didn't arise in my conversation with the conductor.*"

"*Weekends are quality time for us.*"

"*We'll have to spare four out of fifty-two. You could arrange your business trips around my schedule.*"

Stacey stopped folding, giving me her undivided attention. "*You know I have no control over the dates of conferences I attend. When do you start?*"

"*Tomorrow night.*"

"*How much do they pay?*"

"*One hundred dollars per month.*"

"*Why do you always sell yourself short, Alex? You'll spend twice that much on music.*"

"*It's an honorarium, not a salary, and what does it matter? I don't need the money. The amount I make overcharging for jingles should balance out the inequities. Certainly you'd agree that any sum paid for 'Turn your crash into cash' constitutes a gross overpayment.*"

"*All I'm saying is that you deserve more. You don't need to get nasty.*"

"*Likewise.*"

In the hard stare we shared, I knew I'd crossed an unspoken line by surrounding myself with sixty lesbians.

Five dozen potential threats to our relationship.

CHAPTER 11

"Alex!" I called out again. She opened her eyes and turned in my direction. "Am I interrupting something?"

"Kris, come in," she said, sounding almost desperate. "You haven't met my mother, have you?"

"Not yet. I'm Kristin Ashe." I came closer and shook hands, finger-grip only, with the slender woman with coiffed blond hair. She wore a tailored tan suit, black heels and silver costume jewelry, and nothing about her, except the rounded shape of her eyes, resembled Alex.

In repose, her mouth was set in a grim line, but she managed an artificial upturn. "Sharon Madigen. You're the one who's helping Alexandra remember?"

"I am." I bent over the table. "What's this? A photo album?"

"A memory book."

"You made it recently?"

"Oh, no." Sharon caressed the binder with a red fingernail. "I put in the first clipping when Alexandra was seven years old. When she was three years old, I realized she had perfect pitch after hearing her imitate the sounds of crickets chirping. She began piano lessons when she was five, and by six, she could play complex pieces by ear."

I pointed to the glitter and musical notes pasted to one of the pages. "You were ahead of your time, scrapbooking before it became popular."

"I'm glad someone appreciates my intentions." She inclined her head toward her daughter. "I leave the book in her room, but she never opens it unless I'm here."

I sat on the edge of the bed, near Alex. "Can you remember playing the piano?"

"I can't remember a time without it," she said dully.

"In her teens, Alexandra attended prestigious musical camps and performed ten to fifteen concerts per year. The critics called her performances dazzling and her talents prodigious. They said she had a sure touch and emotional depth, that her playing was utterly absorbing. She was featured on the cover of two esteemed classical-music magazines."

"The piano carved away the largest piece of my life, but it wasn't who I was."

"What did you like most about music?" I asked. "Can you remember?"

"The conflict."

"I'll never understand why you dropped out of Juilliard."

Alex leaned back and whispered seductively, "I longed for something more from music, something I found impossible to obtain." To her mother, she said obnoxiously, "I tired of playing the same cycle of pieces. Nothing changed except the degree of my disdain."

Her mother caught my eye. "I think what you're doing for Alexandra is wonderful."

"Thank you. I hope I'm helping."

"If she could remember what a promising life she had, what a gift that would be. We're lucky she's alive."

Alex said, "Luck played no part in it."

"You're right. You've worked hard." Sharon faced me. "She's

learned to feed, dress and groom herself."

"I can tie my shoes, pick dead leaves off live plants and separate square objects from round ones."

Her mother continued as if Alex hadn't spoken. "The first victory came when she squeezed my hand, when she was in the coma. She wouldn't permit me to hold her hand when she was a little girl. She said I held it too tightly. Do you recall?"

"No," Alex said.

"As a child, Alexandra shunned all forms of physical affection. She lived in her own world of music and make-believe. I touched her more when she was in the hospital than I had in the past thirty years. I drank gallons of coffee to endure nights at her side. Do you remember any of that, Alexandra?"

"No."

"When you were unconscious, I massaged your eyebrows. That used to make your pain go away when you were a baby." Sharon switched her attention to me. "The next victory arrived when she opened her eyes and responded to commands. We've celebrated every one since, haven't we?" Alex didn't match her mother's smile or respond. Sharon Madigen went on, undeterred. "Her doctors wouldn't give us a long-term prognosis. In those first weeks, they told us we had to guard against pneumonia, blood clots, infections and collapsed lungs. There was something new to worry about every day." She smiled brightly. "We had hope, though, didn't we? Hope can be the best medicine."

"If it's not the disease," Alex retorted.

"When she regained consciousness, she thought two days had passed, instead of twenty. I wanted to hug her, but she said contact was too painful."

"I'd absorbed the shock of a ninety-one-mile-per-hour crash with my body."

Sharon pretended not to hear her. "She had a tube stuck in her side for three months to drain her liver. She's had microderm abrasion treatments for the scars, but they're still awful, especially the one from the respirator."

I could see Alex tense, and I said, "I didn't notice them when we first met."

Alex shot me a grateful look.

"Her arms and legs are thinner," Sharon said.

"My mother used to model for the Daniels and Fisher department store."

"Then you should know," I said lightly, addressing Sharon. "Thin's always in."

Beyond her mother's apparent notice, Alex and I shared a brief smile.

"People have come up to me at church and said they don't know where I found the strength those first days after the accident."

"It must have been impossibly hard on you."

Sharon ignored Alex's sarcasm. "When my daughter woke up, she asked us to share details of the accident, again and again. I couldn't bear the chore. I left it up to Stacey."

"I was in a daze, Mother."

"But the questions! 'How far did my body fly? What did my car look like? Who was the first person at the scene? Where did I hit the concrete column? When did someone call nine-one-one?'"

Alex said, "It took time for me to conceptualize what had happened."

"That's true. You couldn't recognize words or faces." Sharon turned to me. "She knew nothing about the drive. To this day, she hasn't told us why she was out at that time of night or where she was going."

"You haven't remembered anything?" I asked.

"Only walking for miles before I began to drive."

"Alone?"

Alex met my steady gaze. "Yes."

"Which must be a fantasy," her mother interjected. "You never would have walked after dark."

"I was walking. From daylight into darkness. And sobbing. I couldn't catch my breath."

"That's because you broke your ribs."

"I couldn't breathe *before* I decided to go for a drive."

"Some days, Alexandra thinks more clearly than others."

"Is this one of my good days?" Alex said icily.

"It was."

"I can understand more than anyone knows. I just can't remember."

After an awkward pause, Sharon directed the conversation at me. "When patients are in rehabilitation, most ask to be taken home, but Alexandra never has."

Alex flinched. "I've never asked to go home?"

"Not once."

Another long silence ensued, which for the life of me I couldn't think how to fill, then Alex said, almost under her breath, "New pathways. Stronger connections. Daily regeneration. Improved couplings. That's my mission."

I looked at her quizzically. "In your life?"

"In my brain. I'm rebuilding my brain."

"That's correct, dear," her mother said, seeming somewhat mollified. "Physical and mental gains can continue for up to two years. You should listen to your neurologist. There's no reason to believe you can't improve. Count your blessings your music box wasn't damaged."

"Music box?" I said.

"The area of the brain that regulates musical comprehension," Sharon replied.

"Everything else is shattered. I've lost my independence, and simple tasks require all my concentration, but my genius is intact. It took a week of practice before I could close my hand into a fist." Alex demonstrated by shaking a fist at her mother.

Her mother brushed aside her hand. "When she hears a familiar piece on the radio or one of her discs, she can name the composer, score and orchestra."

"Useless information comes back to me, but I can't control my emotions."

"Music has been part of her recovery. Her doctors marvel at her progress."

Alex's voice rose in frustration. "To me, it's slow, this process of splicing. Why can't anyone understand?"

"I do," I said quietly. "The part of your brain that regulates drive must not have changed. You had intense ambition when you were younger or you wouldn't have achieved what you did musically. You still have it—the desire to excel and the feeling that nothing's ever enough. If you finished tenth in a competition with a thousand people, you'd obsess about the nine ahead of you, not the nine hundred and ninety behind. Something like that?"

Alex stared at me, clearly astonished. "Yes. My music career was like that. I hadn't finished swallowing before I reached for the next sip, and I tasted nothing."

"That's not true," Sharon put in. "You can't remember that."

"How would you know? I explicitly remember living every moment but the one I was living."

"We're so proud of her. Alexandra has survived seventeen surgeries, and with each one, she—"

"—risked coming out more deformed," Alex interrupted.

Her mother made a clucking noise. "With each one, you faced adversity head on."

Alex said tonelessly, "There's risk in every breath we take." Abruptly, she sat up straight and met my eyes. "And an equal amount of heartbreak in the dangers we avoid."

I hadn't yet formed a reply when Sharon said gaily, "You never were afraid. You played Carnegie Hall as if you were born for the stage."

Alex's head snapped around toward her mother. "Before every performance, I became ill. Do you remember that?"

Sharon looked away. "You have a delicate stomach. That comes from your father's side."

"I had to vomit to play, Mother. Does that sound familiar?"

Sharon spoke to me. "Alexandra has changed since the accident."

"Mother's changed, too. She used to make the hand signal for yapping when people talked too much. She doesn't do that anymore, at least not in my presence."

"My daughter is more spiteful."

"I'm less compliant."

"She becomes easily irritated for no reason."

"The reason is traumatic brain injury. Would you like to see the scar on my skull, another one that's so obvious?"

"At least she's showing an interest in music again. She abandoned it fifteen years ago."

"The jingles I wrote didn't count?"

"They were banal."

"The chorus concerts?"

Sharon smiled at me. "Alexandra was a classically trained pianist. You can appreciate the difference, I'm sure, between playing in Carnegie Hall with the finest musicians in the world and playing in a church on Colfax with women who can't carry a tune."

"I didn't know there was a hierarchy in music," I said purposefully.

Alex mouthed a silent thank you.

They think I can't remember, but I can.

This was my second concert in my first season with the chorus, and I felt strangely ill at ease.

How had I come to arrive at this place, at this time?

At the age of five, I'd expressed a naïve interest in the piano, and by eight, I was practicing five hours a day. By ten, I'd become the youngest union member in Colorado, and by fourteen, I'd toured Europe six times with a national symphony. At eighteen, I attended Juilliard on full scholarship, and by twenty, I despised myself. At twenty-two, I left New York, one month shy of graduation, and for the next ten years, I didn't touch the piano.

I waited tables and taught toddlers, but the noise became too much. I painted houses and landscaped yards, grateful for the stillness. I dreamed of becoming a forest ranger, librarian or trash collector, anything but a professional musician, yet somehow I became involved with jingles.

I wrote and recorded catchy phrases that made people feel an attraction. To cars and dog food and political candidates and personal injury lawyers.

I hated what I did, but I couldn't stop doing it.

I was thirty-five before I could play notes again for the sake of music alone.

I was comfortable with the conductor and friendly with the sixty members of the Colorado Lesbian Chorus, but I had no friends.

While I finished last-minute preparations for this spring concert—blouse and skirt pressed, pumps and pearls polished, hair washed, dried and braided, nails trimmed, eyebrows plucked, makeup applied and checked—Stacey called to say that she'd have to miss the concert.

A thirteen-year-old boy had jumped from a balcony on the fifteenth floor of Grant Square, and police officers were on the scene blocking traffic and shepherding onlookers. Firefighters were collecting body parts and hosing down the street. Stacey's job was to comfort, not the mother or father who couldn't be located, but the middle-aged man across the way who saw the teen jump and burst.

She knew I would understand, she said, and I did.

Perfectly.

The performance began, and my anxiety disappeared.

The music consumed me, as it always had.

I sat on my bench, to the side of the stage, and pounded and caressed and strived to connect, and by the end of the three-hour concert, I had nothing left to offer. I was drenched with sweat, and when I bowed, beads of it pooled on the hardwood floor. This concerned me.

I was scheduled to have my picture taken, in concert attire, as soon as the audience departed. The business director wanted snapshots for the group's Web page, and the photographer had worked diligently all night. While I hadn't yet seen her, I'd felt the sting of flashes and sensed her in the shadows. On the risers above and in the pit below, she'd lurked, never far from my consciousness.

When I met her, I decided, I would inform her that she could take but one more shot of me, a single chance to capture something and trap it forever, in paper and chemicals or pixels and toner.

One shot. No more.

Stagehands cleared the area, and the photographer approached.

I stared at her, dumbfounded.

• • •

"Not everyone agrees with me, Kristin." Sharon Madigen's features hardened. "But as I said, what you're doing for Alexandra is wonderful. I've seen nothing but positive changes in my daughter in the last few weeks."

"Such as?" Alex commented vaguely.

"You're more engaged, dear, and the pace of your speech is picking up. Some days, you deign to wear shoes and, thank goodness, you're paying more attention to personal hygiene."

"She means I'm wearing makeup."

"And what's wrong with that?"

"Mother's waiting for my 'miracle day,' when I'll return to who I was. Not the Alexandra before the accident, but the Alexandra at Juilliard. Every time she steps into this room, she searches for someone I never was."

"That's not fair."

Alex went on. "Unfortunately for her, there's no prognosis for traumatic brain injury."

"Which means there are no limitations. You could play the piano again—"

"My fractured skull has healed, leaving people to assume I'm intact," Alex said, almost spitting on her mom, before turning to me. "Nothing could be further from the truth. To all appearances, I'm undamaged. Isn't that ironic? Mother comes to visit me every day, I believe. Don't you, Mother?"

"I haven't missed once since I was summoned to the hospital in the middle of the night."

Alex shuddered. "Did *she* call you?"

"Stacey? Yes, of course she did. You know that."

"Not Stacey."

"Who, dear?"

"I don't know," Alex said, suddenly sounding defeated.

Sharon Madigen flipped to a page in the middle of the memory book and said cheerily, "There you are with your friend from high school. You two were inseparable for a time, but I can't recall her name. Can you? Carissa or Clarissa. Something like that. Peters, I believe. Yes, that's it. Clarissa Peters. You didn't stay in touch, but you told me you saw her again at a chorus concert. Wasn't she a writer or photographer?"

Alex's only response was a low hiss.

They think I can't remember, but I can.

As I gathered sheets of music into a satchel, the photographer approached from the far end of the stage, tendering a slight wave. "Hi, Alex. Remember me?"

I stumbled backward and grabbed the piano to keep from falling. "Er, no," I stammered. "Have we met?"

"Yes, we have. In high school."

"Did we know each other well?"

"Quite."

"Did we like each other?" I asked, attempting humor.

"I hope we did. You kissed me in the bathroom stall after third-period photography. First semester of our senior year."

I couldn't breathe. "You look different."

"I haven't changed that much."

I reached out to shake hands, a movement she turned into a hug. I pulled away quickly, pointing at the camera around her neck. "You're the photographer."

"I am," she said, clearly bemused.

"The business director told me someone would come tonight to take publicity shots, but the name was different. Beth . . . ?"

"Beth Rutherford. She's a friend. I'm filling in as a favor."

In the awkward pause, I fidgeted, Clarissa smiled and I grappled to fill the silence. "You still smile all the time."

"Because everything still amuses me. I have a confession to make. I saw you recently."

My heart heaved in my chest, and I accidentally knocked sheets of music off the stand. I bent to retrieve them. "You did?"

"At the concert last fall. Your performance of the Chopin nocturne was haunting. You deserved the standing ovation."

My shoulders relaxed as I backed up. "Thank you."

"I asked my friend Tamara about you."

I busied myself arranging and rearranging music in the satchel, moving it from compartment to compartment. "What did she say?"

"First, she asked why I was asking. She thought my involvement with another woman should have precluded curiosity."

"But it didn't?"

Clarissa took off the camera's lens cap. "Not at all. Then she told me you were happily involved in a long-term relationship."

"Mmm."

"Ecstatic by all accounts, that there was no chance." She snapped a shot, and I flinched. "I saw your partner come up to you after the concert. She gave you yellow roses, and you two kissed. Is she around?"

"She had to work tonight."

"She better have had a good excuse."

"Stacey's a counselor who works in the coroner's office," I said, my voice becoming higher and higher. "Tonight, a boy jumped from a fifteenth-floor balcony."

Clarissa lowered the camera and shrugged. "That qualifies, I suppose. You know what . . . a few months ago, someone who looked like you came out of my apartment building."

I focused my full attention on the satchel, fumbling with the clasp. "She did?"

"You've never been to the Promenade, on Pearl and Alameda, have you?"

I looked at her and forced a smile. "Never."

"I must have imagined you," she said lightly.

CHAPTER 12

After the visit with Alex and her mother, I returned to my car and checked my voice mail.

No message from Fran, but there was a rambling one from Roxanne Herbert explaining why she hadn't stopped by the office to pick up the tape of my first meeting with her partner, Linda. Her car was in the shop, and would I mind, she'd requested, bringing the tape to her house.

I phoned Roxanne and told her no problem, I was on my way. By the time I'd swung by the office to retrieve the tape and crossed the city in rush-hour traffic, however, I did mind. The seemingly innocuous errand already had consumed more than an hour of nonbillable time, and I pledged to make it brief at Roxanne's. No chitchat or lingering, get in and get out. Better yet, stay out. Hand her the tape on the porch. An excellent idea, except that it didn't work. We wasted ten minutes in the living room talking about her job search, which could have been summarized in two words. *No progress.*

Roxanne had circles under her eyes, tangled hair and an outbreak of acne. "What's on the tape? Should I brace myself?"

"Not necessarily."

"How did Linda act around you?"

"She asked a lot of personal questions."

"That's because we've had problems with renters. She's looking out for our best interests."

"When we went through the house, she always used the word *I*, not *we*. For example, 'I've owned the property for eight years.'"

Roxanne picked at a thread on her tan jogging suit. "Why wouldn't she? She does all the work."

"You haven't contributed?"

"No, and I won't. When we bought the house, I made it clear I didn't want to fix it up or show it to tenants. I was putting in enough hours at Qwest without taking on a part-time job."

"Out of curiosity, did Linda mention that we met?"

"Of course."

"What did she say?"

"That you'd be the ideal tenant."

"Hmm," I said, pleased.

"Don't flatter yourself. She meant that you don't have animals or kids and that you do have a steady job. Did you tell her that you're the principal horn player for the Mile High Orchestra?"

"She might have gotten that idea." I'd followed Fran Green's advice. When constructing an imaginary life, make it an exciting one.

Roxanne said unpleasantly, "My partner did get that idea."

"When you and I first met, you said Linda forms intense attractions to women. Did you notice anything after our meeting?"

Roxanne's answer came too fast. "Not at all."

I took a deep breath, stood and nodded. "That's probably the end of it."

"I'm sure it is."

We walked to the entryway together. "After you listen to the tape, let me know what you want to do. If you'd like, I could ask to see the house again."

"It's been rented," Roxanne replied, the blotches on her face reddening, "and you've done enough already."

Now, what the hell did that mean? I fumed as I drove away, not unaware that Roxanne's car was parked in the driveway.

Weren't she and I on the same side, and why had she lied?

Roxanne could deny Linda was attracted to me, but I knew better. In accordance with the terms of the Test-A-Mate contract, I'd produced an audiotape, but sound alone had captured only a fraction of my interaction with Linda.

The other piece, Roxanne Herbert would never know but I wouldn't soon forget.

As we'd parted on the sidewalk next to my car, Linda Palizzi and I had shaken hands, and the look she'd given me when we touched . . . this wasn't the end of it.

I zipped back to the office, impatient to resolve my dispute with Fran, but she'd knocked off for the day, which disappointed but didn't surprise me. Rarely did she stick around past five, much less until seven.

I looked over a stack of invoices that needed paying and bank statements that needed balancing and decided to avoid them all. Instead, I turned on the computer and used a search engine to direct me to the Colorado Lesbian Chorus's Web site, where I found a wealth of useful information.

First, I identified the conductor of the chorus, Ellen Barry, and sent her an e-mail explaining Alex Madigen's situation. Next, I clicked through at least a hundred photographs, candid and posed shots of individuals and groups at rehearsals and concerts, until I found one of Alex. In the shot, she was playing the piano, head thrown back, eyes tightly closed, mouth open.

Jackpot!

The photograph was credited to Clarissa Peters, the high school friend in the memory book, while all the rest on the Web site had been taken by Beth Rutherford.

I could barely contain my excitement when the phone rang, with Ellen Barry on the line saying she was willing to do anything she could to help. I immediately phoned Alex and confirmed a time that would work for a meeting the next day, before returning to the Web.

I had just clicked on the image of Alex to enlarge it when the door opened and Fran Green tiptoed into the office. "How's it going?" she said gruffly.

"Good. You?"

"Can't complain. Still hot under the collar?"

I wouldn't look at her. "No."

"What happened to us?"

"I don't know. I'm sorry I snapped at you."

"You cranky 'cause you ain't getting any?"

I raised my head. "I might be a little tense with Destiny out of town."

"Welcome to my world, a cold, lonely place."

"Please! You've had more sex in the past year than I'll probably manage in a lifetime."

"True, but enough about me. When's your honey coming home?"

"Not until next Tuesday. What's your excuse for a short temper?"

"Stress. Must have gotten the best of me."

"Stress about what?"

"Worried about the radio show," Fran said, removing her blazer. Aside from a lavender *Dykes Do It Better* T-shirt, she was dressed in all black, down to square-toed shoes. "Started the interview process as a lark. Somewhere along the way, became obsessed with it. Been feeling the need to impart wisdom to quarter-lifers, midlifers, broads my own age. Been on the lookout for the right platform."

"I didn't know the show meant that much to you."

"The world. Strain must have come from performance anxiety. Underwear balled this tight for an interview, can't imagine what it'll feel like when I go live."

"Does that mean . . . ?"

She broke into a broad grin. "Yes, siree. You're looking at Fran Green, spanking-new radio personality."

I stood to hug her. "Congratulations!"

In her exuberance, Fran tried to pick me up in a spin but only succeeded in twisting my spine. "Ice cream sundaes, my treat."

"Not for me. Not if you can't get me off the ground." I rubbed my back. "When do you start?"

"World premiere in three days, Thursday at eleven."

I sat gingerly. "In the morning?"

Fran dropped into her chair and tilted to a dangerous angle. "Nighttime show."

"How will you manage? You hate staying up past nine."

"Try to sleep in on Fridays, past the rooster hour. Won't be easy, but I'll cope. No choice but to adjust, at least until I can work my way up to a prime slot, morning or evening rush hour. You gonna listen in?"

"I wouldn't miss it. What's your topic?"

"Haven't decided, but glue your ear to the speaker, and I'll surprise you."

"Do you want me to call in?"

"If the mood strikes. But can't have you jumping the queue, not ahead of other loyal listeners."

"I understand." I shifted to a more comfortable position, wondering whether our workers' comp policy covered this type of injury. "Back to our disagreement for a second. I understand how you feel about Alex—"

Fran waved dismissively. "Don't listen to me. I was a hothead."

"You did have valid points. I talked to Alex this afternoon and told her you'd be assisting with background checks and research. I explained that you and I are a team, we work well together—"

"Most days," Fran interjected.

"—and that I wouldn't alter our working relationship just because she felt uncomfortable."

Fran nodded. "Appreciate the vote of support. What'd she say?"

"Not much, but I brought up the subject after she'd spent two hours with her mother."

Fran chuckled. "No fight left in her?"

"Exactly."

"Smart move. Give me a job, pronto, before the wunderkind changes her mind."

"Clarissa Peters. I need you to run a background check on her."

Fran lit up and rubbed her hands together. "My specialty. Why her?"

"She and Alex went to high school together. Alex's mom had a picture of the two of them, hanging all over each other."

"Recent?"

"Twenty years old."

"What's up with the time travel?"

"I'm running out of ideas. Alex hired me to reconstruct her life before the accident, but there's not much to reconstruct. She made a living as a jingle writer but hated herself for doing it and had few clients left by the time of her accident. She seemed to want music in her life but couldn't find the answer for it. From early on, her mother pressured her into a career as a classical pianist."

"What's the relationship with the mother like now?"

"Contentious and competitive."

"Not words you like to hear about a mum. How about the primary relationship?"

"Distant. That's how I'd describe Alex and Stacey."

"Happens sometimes with accidents. Trauma can drive a wedge."

"Distant before the crash. Stacey seemed capable of supporting everyone except Alex."

Fran sucked her teeth. "Not good."

"I'm just about out of leads, and from what I've gathered, Alex used to spend an unhealthy amount of time alone. I haven't come up with any hobbies, other than her involvement with the Colorado Lesbian Chorus, or friends, other than Derek Wallace."

Fran whistled softly. "Ain't no surprise the poor gal's short on memories, if she ain't got nothing to remember."

"She has something to remember, but it might not be positive."

"What gives?"

"She's had a dream about a woman, someone with a birthmark on her back. I'm supposed to find her."

"Could be fun," Fran said with a lecherous grin before sobering up. "Think it's this Clarissa chick, the one from high school?"

"Possibly."

"Best go back in time then. Two decades, if necessary."

"Maybe not that far." I swiveled the computer screen until it faced Fran. "Guess who took this picture of Alex at the spring chorus concert, a little over a year ago?"

Fran leaned in, until her nose was within an inch of the image and clapped. "Bravo! Right there in black and white, in the credit line, Clarissa Peters." She raised an eyebrow. "They meet again. By coincidence or design?"

"I don't know."

"Be curious to see what we find in Ms. Peters's background. You want surveillance? I got time. Wouldn't mind tailing her, on my own dime. Need the practice anyway."

"No, no," I said hastily.

"Better yet, how about I attach a GPS locator to her car, track her movements by computer. Let my fingers do the walking as our prey crisscrosses the city."

"Are you serious?"

Fran grinned ear to ear. "Been dying to buy a system since I saw a review in the private-eye magazine. Made me drool."

I rolled my eyes. "How much?"

"Average price, hair over three grand, plus fifty per month for unlimited use."

I gulped. "Three thousand dollars?"

"Worth every bit of coin. Stealth antenna with magnetic attachment installation. Slap that baby on the underbody. Thirty seconds, and it's up, no vehicle entry required. Follow the vehicle live using maps on a Web site, location reports every four seconds. Day and night operation, in all weather conditions. Automatic polling every fifteen minutes gives locations by address and longitude and latitude. Can't beat it for efficiency."

I hesitated. "I don't know."

"You grind it through your gears. Meantime, I'll run background checks on our friend Clarissa, see what she's been up to. Anything else?"

"No," I said distractedly.

Fran snapped her fingers. "Earth to Kris. Something else making you latch on to the mysterious Clarissa?"

"Her expression."

Fran said with exaggerated patience, "Whose? When?"

"Alex, when her mother mentioned Clarissa's name."

"Naked longing?" Fran deduced, laughing.

"Fear," I corrected her. "Naked fear."

The Colorado Lesbian Chorus had sixty active members in it, a fact Ellen Barry, the conductor, reported with pride the next day.

Sixty women, any one of whom, or none of whom, might have the birthmark Alex Madigen had seen in her sexual dream. I could envision Fran Green conducting a lineup at their next rehearsal, checking out the small in women's backs, ecstatic that she'd chosen private investigation as her career after the convent.

I, however, favored a more traditional approach, the garden-variety interview with notetaking.

I was seated next to Ellen Barry at a picnic table under a large cottonwood on the grounds of Sinclair Rehabilitation Center. Sandwiches, chips and soft drinks, which I'd purchased at a nearby deli, rested in front of us, untouched.

"I'm nervous." Ellen smoothed out her black silk pants and ivory, long-sleeve shirt and glanced anxiously at Alex as she made her way toward us. "Will she remember me?"

"Who are you?" Alex shouted from a distance, openly staring at the petite woman in her fifties who had a round face and dark, wavy hair that fell loosely to her shoulders.

"I'm Ellen Barry."

Alex showed no emotion. "How did we know each other?"

"I'm the conductor of the Colorado Lesbian Chorus. You were our accompanist."

"A conductor. Is that all you do?"

"No," Ellen said genially. "I'm an active recitalist and a music teacher in the Metro Denver Public Schools system."

Alex slowly lowered herself to the bench across from us. "Do you play the piano, too?"

"My preferred instrument is the violin."

"What did I do as an accompanist?" Alex said, wiping her forehead, which had beaded with sweat despite an overcast sky and mild temperature.

"At our rehearsals, you warmed up the chorus and ran sectionals. You also wrote arrangements. At our concerts, you accompanied the chorus and played solos."

"Solos?"

"In the fall, you played a Chopin nocturne. For our spring concert, you premiered your own composition, a scherzo, *Agitation*."

Alex looked confused. "I composed something?"

"Yes, and the audience was riveted, as always."

"As always?"

"Magic happened whenever you played."

"What kind of sound did I make?"

"One that was manic and raw. You took the audience with you into another world, on a delightful exploration," Ellen said, her face lit with joy. "You made the music relevant to each individual, and the sheer beauty of your playing was indescribable. On more than one occasion, I burst into tears, and I wasn't the only one."

"How many times did you see Alex play?" I asked.

"Too many to count. I was what you might call a groupie." Ellen laughed self-consciously, then turned back toward Alex. "I first became aware of you at the Vail Valley Music Festival, when you joined the Tri-State Philharmonic. My goodness, what an exhilarating performance, so probing and deeply felt, particularly for a twelve-year-old. You had passion and charisma and brilliant technique. I enjoyed listening to you through the years as you developed your gift. In your teens, your playing became even more deft and spirited."

"You knew me when I was younger?" Alex said, her demeanor

remote.

"Not personally. Only through your music."

"Through it, could you detect my personality?"

Ellen paused in thought. "Somewhat. I remember thinking at the time that I didn't know how you'd fit in with the constraints of the classical ranks. Too many musicians come out of the conservatories overtrained and classical-minded, to the exclusion of everything else."

"I remember feeling apart."

"That you were." Ellen smiled. "You won national and international competitions and played with top orchestras and conductors. If you had desired to do so, you could have been a superstar in the classical world, internationally renowned. You possessed a stunning natural ability."

"Possessed." Alex heaved a sigh. "When I reached my peak, was I alone in the world?"

Ellen nodded. "At the level you achieved in music, there is no competition. Only subjective comparisons."

"I felt isolated," Alex said tonelessly. "Later, when I played with your chorus, what was I like?"

"Consumed, but please don't take that the wrong way. In the music discipline, there are perfectionists at every turn."

"How did we meet, you and I?"

"You e-mailed me and expressed an interest in playing again. I couldn't believe my good fortune. I called you right away and set up a lunch date. I was so pleased to discover that you were coming out of retirement."

Alex cocked her head. "Why had I left music? Do you know?"

"At our first lunch, you shared with me something interesting, that music never had come easily. You didn't enjoy memorizing or practicing. For some pianists, playing is never work, but for you, it was, which surprised me."

"Why?"

"Because your mastery was so complete."

Alex's shoulders slumped. "Ability and desire aren't synonymous."

Ellen smiled sympathetically. "You confided also that music

always had been a struggle between duty and a yearning to be free. The next progression in your career, after you graduated from the conservatory, would have been to tour and record."

"I didn't want to do that?"

"No, especially not the recordings. You couldn't bear the idea of leaving behind permanent sounds."

"There were no other opportunities?"

"Oh, certainly. You could have held a position as a rehearsal pianist for a dance company or ballet or opera."

"None of that interested me?"

"No, and at your level, it shouldn't have."

"I had no other options?"

"You could have taught piano."

"But that would have required connecting with people?"

Ellen gave Alex a puzzled look. "Yes, of course."

"Thank you for telling me why I left music. I've asked my mother repeatedly, but she won't answer."

"I'm sure she must have been disappointed—"

Alex cut in, "Why did I come back to it?"

"You wanted an outlet for your passion."

"Did I?"

"That's what you shared with me, and certainly, you made up for lost time. At the spring concert, as I said, your scherzo was breathtaking. We missed you at the cast party. Everyone wanted to offer congratulations. I wish you'd been there, as part of the group."

"Where was I?"

"I don't know where you went. You were scheduled to have your picture taken for the Web site, and that's the last I saw of you."

Alex peered at Ellen. "Did I know the photographer?"

"You did. Clarissa Peters. She was filling in for our usual photographer, Beth Rutherford. By chance, she was a friend from high school, someone you'd lost touch with. Perhaps you stayed behind to catch up on old times. It's a small world, isn't it?"

"Intimate," Alex said absentmindedly.

• • •

They think I can't remember, but I can

We were the only ones left in the theater, and I couldn't catch my breath.

She posed me for a formal portrait, seating me on the piano bench and positioning my body. I clasped my hands tightly to hide their trembling, and she backed up and took a few shots.

"How's your mom?" she asked. "Still hovering?"

"Not anymore. I've disappointed her enough times that she's left me alone. How are your parents?"

"Super. They retired to Arizona last year."

"And your brother?"

She tilted the camera. "He's an asshole. A gun-toting Republican bigot."

"He hasn't changed," I observed, and we shared a smile that made me ache.

"Turn your head slightly to the left."

I complied. "Do you do this professionally, photography?"

"Only as a hobby. For a living, I make prosthetics."

"Interesting."

She shrugged. "It pays the bills, but this is my passion. I get lost in the images."

"I can see that. Did you go to Yale, like you'd always dreamed?"

"I never attended college. Life interrupted. You?"

"I went to Juilliard but never graduated."

She moved in, close enough for me to feel her breath, and I couldn't stop shaking.

She circled around, reeling off shots from various angles, after which she knelt in front of me to make micro adjustments to my legs and skirt. Before she could rise for the next shot, I reached down and touched a strand of her hair. At this, she looked up, then lowered her head and began to cry.

"We'll break each other's hearts again."

I can't remember whether I said that or she did.

CHAPTER 13

"I'm so pleased Kristin contacted me," Ellen Barry said cheerfully.

Alex blinked rapidly, erasing a blank stare. "Are you?"

"Some of the chorus members heard that you'd been in an accident, but no one could get in touch. It's so good to see you. I wish the group were here. They'd love to get reacquainted. We're performing in two weeks, after the Gay Pride parade. I'd be honored to have you as my guest, if you can make it."

"I'm sure I can't."

"Whenever you feel up to it, we'd welcome you in any capacity. Perhaps you and Shelly could share duties. I know she wouldn't mind."

"Shelly?"

"Shelly Thompson, our accompanist."

"Did she take over after Alex's accident?" I asked.

Ellen said reluctantly, "A short time before."

"Why?" I blurted out, a beat before Alex could.

"I'm so sorry, Alex, but I had to find someone I could rely on. Shelly had been kind enough to fill in when you missed rehearsals. I didn't want to leave a message on your voice mail. I would have preferred to tell you in person, but I was acting in the best interest of the chorus . . ." Ellen's voice trailed off.

"Not in my interest?"

"I was afraid we'd arrive at the hour of the performance and you'd disappear again."

Alex began to breathe shallowly. "Disappear?"

"For weeks, you'd been coming to rehearsals late, and eventually, you skipped them altogether."

"Did that matter, the lead-up to the climax?"

"Very much."

"I must have had a reason. Did you consider that?"

"If you did, you wouldn't share it. When I inquired about personal issues, you changed the subject. I wondered if your disposition had anything to do with Clara Schumann."

"Who is she, one of the members of the chorus?" I asked.

Ellen laughed gently. "She was a pianist and composer, one of the best of the Romantic Era. The last time I saw you, Alex, you asked if I felt Clara had suffered enough for her betrayal."

Alex blanched but didn't speak.

"I'm not following," I said.

"Alex was fascinated by the love triangle of Clara, her husband, Robert, and Johannes Brahms." Ellen reached across the table to touch Alex's hand, and Alex recoiled. "I'm sorry about the way we left things. I tried everything I could to get through to you the night of the dress. You weren't answering your phone. I couldn't come up with a better solution than to tell you in a message on your cell phone."

"When was this, the dress rehearsal?" I asked.

"August sixteenth."

Alex began to shake, and I gasped. "You're sure about the date?"

Ellen nodded. "It was three days before our summer concert."

"The date of my accident," Alex said, faltering.

"What time did you leave the message on Alex's voice mail?"

"Around six, shortly after dress was scheduled to begin."

"Do you remember receiving Ellen's message?"

Alex clutched at her hair. "I was preoccupied."

They think I can't remember, but I can.

Clarissa was lying on her back on the couch, hands behind her head, while I sat rigidly on a chair next to her. Sheets of rain were falling, streaking her apartment window.

"I'd love to meet Stacey," she said.

"That's not possible."

"Why?"

"Stacey works unpredictable hours."

"But that's not why you won't introduce us, is it?"

"No."

"How long have you been together?"

"Eleven years."

"Where did you meet?"

"At a community garden. We had plots next to each other."

"What did you grow?"

"Strawberries." I was past the point of small talk. "Can I ask your advice on something?"

"Of course."

"I'm afraid I'm falling in love with someone."

Clarissa rolled onto her side for a better view of me. "Does Stacey know?"

"No."

"Does the other woman know?" She lowered her voice. "I assume it's a woman."

I held her gaze, careful not to move a muscle. "Yes, she's a woman, and no, I don't think she knows."

"What advice do you need?"

I took a deep breath, releasing it in a prolonged exhale. "Have you been in that situation?"

"Which one specifically?"

"Had feelings for someone who was off limits?"
Her eyes narrowed. "Yes."
I noticed my hands shaking slightly. "What did you do?"
"Nothing."
"Did you regret it?"
"The feelings?"
"The passivity."
"Yes, I do."
"Not did?"
"Do," she said quietly.
"What should I do?"
Clarissa flipped onto her back, placed her hands behind her head and stared at the ceiling. "I can't answer that, Alex."

"At times, I wish they hadn't saved me," Alex said numbly as we watched Ellen Barry cross the lawn.

"Why?"

"Do you have any more visits planned, with these strangers from my past?"

"Not yet, but I'd like to track down Clarissa Peters."

"Who?"

"The photographer who took your picture at the spring concert, your friend from high school. Do I have your permission?" I asked belatedly, already having assigned the task to Fran.

"Do whatever you want."

"Do you remember Clarissa? Could she be the woman in your dreams?"

Alex rose. "I have to go. I'm late for physical therapy."

"Did you complete the sketch of the birthmark?"

"No, I didn't," Alex called out from twenty paces away. "Whoever she is, she doesn't matter to me anymore."

They think I can't remember, but I can.
Days passed, and we exhausted ourselves with meaningless phone

conversations until, once again, we met in her apartment. We sat on opposite ends of the couch, facing the middle and each other. Clarissa had her legs extended, and I was curled in a loose ball, knees touching my chest.

"Aren't you curious whether I'm involved with someone?" she said.

"Not particularly."

"Well, I am. Her name is Leah Stark. She's a bartender and theatrical set designer. She's quite a bit younger than I am, and we've been dating for three months."

"I see."

"Would you like to know if it's serious?"

"No."

"It's not. I go to extremes to avoid anything serious. Do you want to know how we met? She picked me up at a bar."

"In Oblivion," I said involuntarily.

Clarissa leaned forward and gave me a peculiar look. "How did you know?"

"A guess."

"I had the strangest feeling all day, as if I would meet someone."

"Can I ask you something, and will you answer honestly?"

"Maybe."

"The second I stop speaking, you'll reply?"

She nodded and smiled. "Sure."

I jammed myself against the arm of the couch and took a deep breath. "Are you attracted to me?"

She blushed and retracted her legs. "You know I can't answer that."

"Why?"

"Because if I do, we'll go somewhere we shouldn't."

The silence between us cradled more pain than I ever could have imagined. Without making a sound or movement, I began to cry. "You're right."

She reached over to touch my arm. "I'm unbelievably attracted to you, but you know that or you wouldn't have asked."

"I suppose," I whispered, staring straight ahead, unwilling to let go.

"I could torment your conscience by asking the same question, but I won't."

My heart raced. "Why?"

Clarissa leaned forward, cupped my moist cheek in her hand and tilted her head to meet my eyes. "Because every time I'm near you, I feel the answer."

Too aggravated to traipse after Alex, I packed up the leftovers and folded the plastic tablecloth.

Look for a woman with a birthmark on her back. Don't look for her. What was I supposed to do?

This was no easy task, taking instructions from a client with a brain injury, and I had begun to agree with Stacey Wilhite, Alex's ex-partner. Undoubtedly, Alex could remember more than she let on, but if so, why had she hired me? Perhaps she needed help admitting she remembered. Toward that end, what could I do other than continue to probe all facets of her life?

I placed a call to Fran Green, who answered on the first ring. "What's up?"

"I need you to find out everything you can about Clara Schumann, Robert Schumann and Johannes Brahms."

"Names ring a bell."

"They were pianists and composers who lived in Germany during the nineteenth century. Ellen Barry said Alex was fascinated by them."

"Will do. How'd the meeting go?"

"I'll fill you in when I get back. Have you eaten lunch?"

"Couple bites of a Luna bar," Fran said, which explained her gravelly voice. "What'd you have in mind?"

"No one touched the food I brought. I'll be back in thirty minutes."

"Picnic in the office. Sounds good! Speed it up!"

Speed it up, I thought, exiting the grounds of Sinclair, pondering what I could have missed in my search for Alex Madigen's memories. I suspected the answers lay in the questions she asked, which meant I'd need to isolate her words for study.

There was only one way to do that—tape-record her.

With her permission?

No. I decided she was guarded as it was.

I'd have to capture her secretly.

How could I have survived a childhood mired in secrecy, only to earn my living through stealth?

That night, I couldn't escape the irony as I lay on my bed with my clothes on and watched through the skylight as a half moon, shrouded in fog, traveled across the sky.

The next morning, I awoke to a light drizzle, still tormented about my plan to covertly record Alex.

In Colorado, it was completely legal to secretly tape-record a conversation, as long as one party to the conversation consented. I qualified as the consenting party, but was it ethical? Without ever fully answering that question, I tucked the Olympus recorder into one of the pockets of my loose-fitting khakis.

I went straight from home to Sinclair and found Alex Madigen seated at the table in her room, next to a young woman who was extolling the virtues of aromatherapy.

Dressed in an orange floral skirt and lemon tube top, Alex's guest modulated her voice with every feature of the healing potions spread out before her. She'd wrangled most of her wavy hair into a braid that rested between her shoulder blades, but loose ends sprung out in every direction, and her hair clip bulged to the point of breakage. She smiled frequently, in the likeness of a five-year-old prompted to say "cheese," and from my angle, she looked to be no older than twelve. I assumed she was one of the volunteers who visited the rehab center on a regular basis, and for a minute, I simply observed as she gibbered about the properties and synergies of essential oils and Alex nodded politely, if dazedly.

No mystery why she was dazed. The smell of rose, lemon and lavender was enough to overpower anyone.

When I interrupted with a hearty "hello," Alex lurched forward in relief, and her companion looked up to eye me with curiosity. After brief introductions, Leah Stark excused herself to fetch audiotapes from her car, and the instant she was out of earshot, Alex whispered, "Why did you send this bizarre person to me?"

I froze in my reach for one of the tiny bottles. "I didn't. I've never met her. Who is she?"

"I don't know, but I want her to go away."

"Why haven't you asked her to leave?"

"I refuse to give her that much power."

"You don't remember her at all?"

"She told me we shared a friend." Alex shoved everything off the table into a grocery bag. "But that can't be true."

"How did she find you?"

"She claims to know someone in the chorus. At their rehearsal last night, Ellen Barry broadcast my predicament to the group, and I haven't had a moment of peace since." Alex gesticulated wildly at the flowers and gift baskets that filled the room. "They're drowning me in kindness."

"Why did the receptionist let Leah through?" I said, all too willing to blame my nemesis, Holly, who was on duty at the front desk.

"Holly had no way of knowing this person would distress me, but I'll certainly tell her."

"What are the tapes Leah's talking about?"

"Some drivel about spirituality and healing. She insists I listen to them. They'll speed my recovery, she promises."

"Hmm."

Alex looked toward the doorway with loathing. "A promise she can't possibly keep."

They think I can't remember, but I can.

I didn't feel like eating a single bite.

How could I have?

I was sitting in an Italian restaurant with Clarissa and her girlfriend.

And Stacey.

Clarissa and I were on one side of a booth, sharing the middle. Stacey and Leah were on the other side, far apart.

Clarissa and Leah reached across the table to feed each other, trading bites of rosemary chicken and spinach ravioli.

I looked away.

"Where did you two meet?" Stacey asked.

Leah giggled. "In Oblivion."

Stacey looked confused, and I added, "The nightclub."

"Did you know you were attracted to each other right away?"

"I did," Leah said, "but I could hardly get near Clarissa. Women were hitting on her, and I saw her reject at least three."

Clarissa smiled. "You exaggerate."

Leah shook her head, sending frizzy hair flying. "I was afraid I didn't have a chance, especially after that girl tried to give you her phone number."

Clarissa wiped her lips with a cloth napkin. "She wasn't my type."

"This Barbie doll approached Clarissa and said, 'If I give you my phone number, will you call?' and Clarissa said, 'No.' I didn't want the same thing to happen to me, but I knew I had to trust the universe."

"What did you do?" Stacey asked.

"I came up and said, 'If I give you my phone number,' and before I could finish, Clarissa said, 'Your cell phone?'"

I muffled a gasp as Clarissa touched me under the table, a lingering, deliberate stroke.

"Yes." Leah flashed a flirtatious smile toward Clarissa.

"Do you have it with you?" Clarissa said, reenacting the scene.

"Always."

"Get ready to answer it."

I shifted uncomfortably, and Stacey clapped her hands in delight.

Leah sighed. "We spent that first night together. My favorite part was snuggling in bed and watching the snow fall."

"It sounds like a fairy tale," Stacey said.

"I couldn't stop smiling. Remember that, Clarissa?"

"How did you feel the morning after?" I asked, surprised by the sound of my own voice. "How did you feel when you had to drive away?"

Leah frowned. "Actually, I had to call a cab because someone had hit my truck and bent the wheel well."

"Did they leave a note?" I said innocently.

Leah stopped picking through the remnants of the fried calamari she'd ordered for the table and looked at me directly. "No, but karma will catch up to them."

"I offered to pay for the repair," Clarissa said.

"Why?" Stacey interjected. "You weren't responsible."

"In a way, I was."

I studied Clarissa with interest, wondering, not for the first time, how much she knew. "Really?"

She met my gaze. "I should have had Leah park in the lot. You never know who's out there, lurking in the streets."

Leah returned a few minutes later. "Here they are. If you listen to the tapes, they'll open you to the possibilities of the universe. I included chants, meditations and affirmations, with Native American flute music in the background."

"Thank you."

"I was wondering, Leah," I said casually, "how do you know Alex?"

"Like I told Alex, we have a mutual friend. Remember, Alex? Clarissa Peters. You know Clarissa." Leah turned to face me, revealing a hostility in her eyes that contradicted her upbeat tone. "Clarissa and I hooked up last year, but we weren't compatible energy-wise. When we were together, I met Alex and Stacey."

"You know Stacey?" Alex said, obviously startled.

"Don't you remember? The four of us went to dinner at Mario's."

Alex shook her head vehemently. "No."

"Are you still in touch with Clarissa?" I asked.

"We're buds. Don't worry, Alex, I don't blame you for anything."

"Blame her?" I said, puzzled when Alex didn't speak.

"We would have broken up anyway. Clarissa and I weren't meant to be, but we learned the lessons we were meant to learn. Totally," she added bitterly.

"What are you talking about—" I began.

"I don't need to call up that negative energy again."

"I don't understand—" Alex broke off when Leah moved in to hug her.

"It was great seeing you," Leah said in a grand voice, seemingly unaware that Alex hadn't returned the embrace. "I can't tell you how light I feel. This was incredibly cleansing!"

I said, "Nice meeting you."

"You, too." Leah reached into her large canvas purse and handed Alex a decorative envelope. "I almost forgot, Clarissa's opening a show tonight at her new studio. You should come."

I watched as Alex opened the invitation. "What type of show?"

"Nature photography. I helped her with the displays, and we separated the artwork by winter, spring, summer and fall. It's really amazing!"

"Nature shots?" Alex said bleakly.

"Waterfalls, wildlife, mountain peaks and sunsets from around Colorado, in the most vibrant colors. You wouldn't believe how prolific and creative Clarissa has been this year. She's opened up and grown, technically and aesthetically. It must be her time to shine. Come and you can meet her girlfriend, Pamela. You don't have to worry, Alex. Clarissa's friends are loving and accepting."

"Girlfriend?" Alex whispered.

"Can you travel?" Leah projected her voice. "Do they let you out?"

"Not readily."

"It's not a prison," I said, speaking over Alex.

Leah flashed a perfunctory smile. "Anyway, think about it. Clarissa talks about you all the time. Should I tell her to look for you?"

"No, please, no," Alex said in an agitated tone. She touched the depression on the back of her head. "I'm afraid that wouldn't be possible."

CHAPTER 14

They think I can't remember, but I can.

Clarissa and I had separated, and the three of them were on their fourth bottle of wine.

Stacey and Leah had moved closer together. I was pushed back against the side of the booth, as far from Clarissa as possible, but she had her arm stretched across the cushion, almost touching my shoulder. The bill for our dinner was tucked under her leg.

Leah gestured at Clarissa and me. "Did you two have a thing back in high school?"

Clarissa started to speak, but I overpowered her. "No!"

"You were just friends?"

"Close friends," Clarissa replied.

"You didn't stay in touch?" Stacey asked.

"No. Alex left school a semester early."

Stacey raised her eyebrows. "I didn't know that. Why?"

"Because I had enough credits to graduate."

"*You must have hated high school as much as I did,*" Leah said.

I pushed away the Styrofoam container that held all but three bites of the seared halibut I'd ordered. "*Quite the opposite, actually.*"

Stacey stared at me strangely. "*What did you do with your free time, before you left for Juilliard?*"

"*Lay in bed all day.*"

"*Didn't you miss your friends?*" *Leah asked.*

My eyes stung. "*With all my heart.*"

"*You and Clarissa would have been hot together,*" *Leah declared, pointing her wineglass at us.* "*The piano prodigy and the soccer star.*"

Clarissa smiled. "*I barely made the varsity team.*"

"*Let it go, Leah,*" *I added harshly.*

"*Clarissa claims you won a national music competition.*"

"*Two,*" *I corrected.* "*And an international one.*"

"*I didn't know that either,*" *Stacey said, her tone implying betrayal.* "*I knew you toured Europe, but you never mentioned a competition.*"

"*It was a long time ago.*"

"*Not when we met, it wasn't,*" *Stacey protested.*

"*Then in particular, I couldn't stand to focus on it. If people knew I played the piano, that became their singular interest, causing all other parts of myself to disappear.*"

"*But you had an extraordinary gift.*" *Stacey said, seeming almost belligerent.*

"*Talent I never fully exploited.*"

"*You're still talented, Alex,*" *Stacey said.* "*It's just that you use your talent in a different way.*"

I sang, "*Turn your crash into cash.*"

Leah snickered. "*You did an ad for that cheesy lawyer, the one who's on late-night cable?*"

"*Yes.*"

"*I hate that tune. I hear it all the time, and I can't get it out of my head.*"

I moved my gaze lazily from Stacey to Leah. "*That's the point.*"

Stacey, knowing me well enough to sense rising anger, directed an inquiry at Clarissa. "*Did you hear Alex play?*"

"*Several times.*"

"What was she like?"

"The same as now, obsessed."

I smiled wryly. "I haven't changed at all?"

Clarissa shifted in the booth to face me directly. "You have. You're more passionate. You must know it matters this time. At the spring concert, it felt different, like you were frantic to connect with someone in the audience. Anyone." Clarissa turned her head toward Stacey. "Did you notice that, too?"

"I didn't attend Alex's last concert. I had to work that night."

"What a shame. Did Alex show you the photographs I took of her?"

"She did. I plan to frame one and hang it in our bedroom."

"Which one?"

"At the moment, I can't recall."

"Overall, what did you think of the photos?"

"You have a professional eye," Stacey said, stilted.

"But did I capture your partner's radiance?"

"How would I know if I wasn't there?"

An awkward silence followed, which Leah filled. "You were blessed to bump into each other. Clarissa was sick all day, and I didn't want her to go to the concert. Remember, sweetie? I made you chicken soup and put cold compresses on your head."

"I wasn't that ill," Clarissa objected.

"You were, too, but you insisted on going. You said it was your only opportunity. That makes it extra auspicious that you two met again."

My head throbbed as I considered this new information, and I couldn't look at any of them.

Not Stacey or Leah.

Especially not Clarissa.

After Leah Stark left, I waited for Alex to open her eyes.

"I can't trust myself or my reactions," she said softly. "I need the truth. Answer me honestly. Promise me you will."

"All right."

"Did that woman dislike me?"

"Intensely."

We both laughed, a nervous release. "Why, do you suppose?"

"You don't remember having dinner with her at Mario's?"

"No, and why would I choose to spend time with such a strange person? What have I done to her? I have no recollection."

"Who knows, but you better not listen to her spirituality tapes," I kidded. "She might have planted negative messages in them."

Alex tossed the cassettes toward the trash, missing the bin. "I have enough of those circulating in my head."

"Forget Leah. Do you remember Clarissa?"

"I believe I do. In high school, I had a friend named Clarissa, didn't I?"

"Yes. Do you know why you lost touch?"

"We lost everything when we touched," she said, her eyes locked in a distant stare. "I also remember someone named Clarissa taking my picture after a performance."

"The spring chorus concert," I agreed. "Ellen Barry mentioned that yesterday."

"Ellen Barry?"

"The conductor of the chorus."

"Yes," Alex said vaguely. "Is it possible these two women named Clarissa are the same person, someone who came to me once and then again?"

"Ellen thought so. What are your memories of Clarissa?"

"I don't know if the clips I see belong to me," she said after a moment's pause. "From the life I left behind."

My pulse quickened. "What do you see?"

"I can't move," Alex whispered, the color draining from her face.

"What's happening?"

Her voice quaked. "She touched me, and . . ."

"And?" I prompted gently.

"I held her breath."

They think I can't remember, but I can.

I was on the toilet, fully clothed, rocking back and forth. Clarissa opened the stall door, came in and crouched in front of me.

I looked up, anguished. "You can't come in here."

"We have to talk."

I put my head in my hands. "We've been talking. For two hours."

"I had to see you."

"I was right next to you."

"Alone."

"This dinner was an awful idea."

"Why did you arrange it?"

"Because I thought if I brought you and Stacey together, I could avoid tearing myself apart."

"I can't do the couples thing anymore, Alex. It's driving me crazy to be polite, as if nothing happened between us."

"Nothing did happen, and what didn't happen was a long time ago. What does it matter?"

"We have to talk about it."

"I don't want to talk."

"Why not? Aren't you happy in your relationship with Stacey?"

"Ecstatic."

"And I'm happy with Leah."

"According to you."

"What are you so afraid of? The past can't hurt us anymore."

"It will never stop hurting us."

She started to hug me. "Please, talk to me."

I removed her hands. "I need to get back to the table."

Neither of us moved. "Please, Alex."

I wiped away tears. "I can't be alone with you. Not ever again."

Whatever Alex Madigen could remember, she wouldn't say that day.

I left shortly after the strange "I held her breath" declaration, grateful to have tape-recorded every word of our conversation. Back at the office, I replayed the forty-minute tape, pausing frequently to take notes. Midway through the third hearing, the front door opened, and Fran Green entered, clad in black galoshes and a yellow rain slicker.

She shook moisture off a red umbrella built for two, spraying me with drops. "Boy, you opened a can of worms with these Germans."

"What Germans, and where have you been?"

Fran propped the umbrella against the wall. "Music library at the college, reading up on Clara Schumann, Robert Schumann and Johannes Brahms. You having memory problems? You gave me the assignment."

"I thought you were doing a background check on Clarissa Peters."

"Unball your undies. Spent the better part of yesterday digging, but can't rush the reports. You know that. Should have a verbal ready by end-of-business today or first thing tomorrow. Where's the fire?"

"Clarissa has a photography show opening tonight, and I plan on being there."

"Good move. Free food and booze. You want company?"

"No, I can manage."

"You're the boss. Meantime, you want to hear about the maestros while they're fresh in my mind?"

I nodded. "Please tell me you found parallels between Alex Madigen's life and Clara Schumann's."

"Yep." Fran inserted a CD into a player on her desk and sat on the edge of mine. "Let's start with the prodigy angle. Clara's father Friedrich Wieck owned a piano store and taught the instrument. Parents divorced when Clara was five, and father took custody. Made young Clara learn pieces by ear. Had her practicing, studying language and music theory, attending concerts. She played publicly at the ripe age of nine and toured Paris with solo recitals at eleven."

"Wow!" I said, impressed.

Fran removed a small notebook from her slicker pocket and flipped it open. "Hold on for more. The wunderkind grew up to become one of the most famous pianists of her era. Among the first to play memorized recitals." She pressed a remote, upping the volume on the classical piece. "Check this out."

"What is it?"

"*Piano Concerto in A Minor*. Clara started composing it when she was fourteen and performed it at sixteen. With the Leipzig

Gewandhaus orchestra, conducted by Felix Mendelssohn," Fran said, butchering the names.

"When did Clara meet Robert Schumann?"

"Getting to that," Fran shouted over the sound before pausing the disc. "Strange tale there. Robert moved into the Wieck household, came in as a piano student and boarder when he was twenty and Clara was eleven. When she was nineteen, they tried to get married, but Papa withheld permission. Lovebirds had to sue for the right."

"Why did Clara's father object to the marriage?"

"Robbie was a womanizer and heavy drinker. Talented pianist and composer, but no prize as a hubbie."

"They must have married at some point."

"Did indeed. Won the court battle and tied the knot the day before Clara's twenty-first birthday."

"Were Clara and Robert happy together?"

"Not entirely. Clara had to curtail her career. Couldn't practice, compose and perform at the same clip. Robert wanted her to give up the calling, stay home and breed. But that wouldn't have worked, 'cause he couldn't provide for ten."

I raised an eyebrow. "They had eight children?"

"Seven or eight. We'll go with eight. Top that off with health problems, and life wasn't what you'd call romantic. Rheumatoid arthritis, controlled with opium, for her. Partial paralysis of the right hand and manic depression for him. Fourteen years into the marriage, he threw himself into the Rhine on a cold day in February. When that didn't kill him, voluntarily traipsed off to an asylum. Died there two years later."

"How tragic!"

"Doesn't begin to describe it. Bring in Johannes Brahms, and this one's a five-star weeper."

"Clara and Johannes had an affair?"

"Hard to say." Fran scratched her chin. "Sexual, doubtful. Emotional, you bet. This fella Brahms entered the picture when he was twenty and carried a torch for Clara till the day he died. Never married, her or anyone else. Clara was thirty-four and Robert was forty-three when the triangle first formed. Next thing you know,

Robert started mentoring Johannes, all but adopted him, touted him as music's greatest hope."

"Another Clara creation?" I asked, referring to the new piece of music playing.

"*Brahms Alto Rhapsody*. Rumor had it, Jo wrote this baby as a wedding gift for the woman he loved but never married, Clara Schumann."

"Clara and Johannes didn't get together after Robert died?"

"Officially, no, but they were bosom buddies for decades, right up until she kicked the bucket at seventy-five. Johannes died less than a year later. Supposedly liver cancer felled him. Bet you anything, it was a broken heart."

"Are you crying?"

"Speck of dust," she said gruffly, rubbing both eyes. "If someone cleaned around here, we wouldn't be subjected to these workplace hazards."

"Mmm-hmm. Could you turn that down?" I said as the music reached a crescendo.

"No problem." Fran flicked the remote. "Tell you what I learned in all this, and it ain't got nothing to do with illicit relationships. Classical music is powerful stuff, like a drug."

"You believe this theory relates to Alex?"

"Yes, ma'am. When the music was gone, what obsession replaced it?" Fran's head bobbed up and down, and her eyes narrowed. "Chew on that for a while."

I frowned. "Talk about a downer."

"I'm just saying." Fran shrugged. "You want to get to the bottom of your pseudo-amnesia mystery, follow the obsession."

Before I could respond to Fran's pronouncement, notes pealed from the vicinity of my feet. "Do you hear church music?"

"*Pachelbel's Canon*, and it's coming from your desk," Fran said in a stage whisper. "You change the ringer on your phone?"

"Oh, shit." I dove for the bottom drawer. "It's the spare."

I retrieved the cell phone Fran had given me for the decoy case and clutched it, dumbstruck. I couldn't find the talk button.

Fran responded to my paralysis. "Give it here."

"I can do it." I pushed a button. "Hello."

"Kris?"

"Yes?"

"This is Linda Palizzi. I hope I'm not interrupting anything."

"I was leaving for a, ah, for a rehearsal."

"I won't keep you, but I wanted to see if we could meet again."

I swear, I could hear the easy smile in her voice. Meanwhile, I saw a curious one on the face across the desk from me. I covered the phone and muttered, "Could I have a little privacy?" Fran didn't move, and her smile grew with my discomfort. I uncovered the phone and spoke in to it. "Meet?"

"I rented the house in Bonnie Brae to a doctor and her husband, but I have something else in your price range. Eleven hundred for a house in Belcaro, on South Garfield Street."

"Belcaro?"

"Could we meet for drinks?"

"Drinks?"

"I have tenants in the property and can't show it just yet, but I'd love to see you again."

"Again?" This was like a bad dream. All I could do was parrot, one measly word at a time.

"How about Friday at eight o'clock, at Rollo's on South Gaylord?"

My "Friday?" must have sounded like an accord, because Linda said, "Fantastic! See you then," and disconnected.

I stared ahead, not quite sure what to make of the conversation.

Fran snapped her fingers to get my attention. "That the target? She on the hook? Give!"

"Give?" The mimicry continued.

"Get a grip, kiddo. Don't fold on me now."

I tucked my shaking hands below my thighs. "What have I done?"

CHAPTER 15

That evening, thoughts of Linda Palizzi and her potential for cheating all but vanished, replaced by a fixation on Clarissa Peters.

I couldn't stop staring at her.

In the fifteen minutes since I'd arrived at her studio on Santa Fe Drive, I had yet to work up the courage to approach her. From an alcove by the temporary bar, I could only watch as she greeted guests and accepted congratulations on the opening of her photography show.

Twenty examples of her extraordinary camera work were displayed in the long, narrow space. The smaller pictures had been placed on cubes on the white-painted wood floor, while the larger ones were attached to exposed brick walls or suspended from the tall, timbered ceiling. Track lights dangling from silver wires created an unsettling atmosphere of focused brightness and splayed darkness.

Seemingly unaware of my study, Clarissa moved around the room with ease.

Long-limbed and slender, she'd dressed casually for the occasion, in stone-colored cropped pants, a tight-fitting olive tank top and leather sandals. Her shoulder-length dark brown hair was streaked with blond highlights, brushed up and away from her face, and she had a tendency to turn to one side when she addressed people, the stance highlighting an angular nose and high cheekbones. Her intense eyes seemed to measure everything and everyone, a habit I found fascinating.

"You came!" a voice said, breaking into my thoughts, causing me to jump.

"Leah," I replied guiltily.

"I had a premonition you would. Doesn't this space have the coolest vibe?"

"It's striking."

"How do you like my artistic look?"

"Mmm," I said, unable to react positively to Leah Stark's braided pigtails, blown-forward shag bangs, Gatsby hat or gunnysack dress.

"Clarissa finally listened to the Tarot cards and sold her reconstruction business last month. It was about time!"

"Reconstruction?"

"She used to make body parts, but that was depleting her. She's entering a new life cycle, and she needs all her energy. This is so the right move for her. Have you two met?"

"Not yet."

"Come on. I'll introduce you."

I waved her off. "She's busy. This is a big night for her."

"Get over yourself." Leah grabbed my arm and tugged me across the room, caroming us off clusters of people along the way. "Clarissa, darling, this is Kristin . . ." she said, interrupting Clarissa's instructions to one of the circulating waiters.

"Ashe," I said, filling in the obvious gap.

The waiter scurried off, and Clarissa faced me head-on before moving in for a glancing hug. "Kristin, thank you so much for coming."

"Kristin was with Alex when I stopped in to visit her," Leah said.

Clarissa searched the room. "Is Alex with you?"

"She wasn't feeling up to it."

"I'm sorry to hear that."

"I told you she wouldn't come," Leah said peevishly, spinning around to view the bar. "I need a drink. You're on your own. 'Bye."

After Leah's departure, Clarissa adopted a placating tone. "You'll have to forgive my ex-girlfriend's rude behavior. She's young."

"You don't need to apologize."

"Leah wants that big cat for a pet," she said, carelessly pointing to a once-in-a-lifetime shot of a mountain lion in full stride, crossing a meadow filled with aspens. "Or maybe a fox. She hasn't decided which. That's all you need to know to understand Leah."

"I don't see you two together."

"Neither did I, but I like variety. We need to get you a drink. Wine, beer, mixed cocktail. Name your preference."

"Nothing, thanks. I have trouble walking, talking and sipping at the same time."

"I know what you mean, but that's usually at the end of my evenings, not the beginning."

I smiled and gestured at the crowd, which had thickened since I'd arrived. "This is impressive, a full house."

She batted her eyelashes and gave a slight bow. "It humbles me."

"Is this your first show?"

"Sixth, but it feels as nervewracking as my first."

"You should relax. Your photographs are spectacular."

"What do you like about them?"

"The grace and isolation."

Clarissa laughed quietly, an intimate sound. "Most people say something about the colors, because they see images. You see the meaning behind the images. Which one's your favorite?"

"I love the owl on the lodgepole pine."

"I do, too. Aren't owls extraordinary creatures? They have an air of detachment, which I find engaging."

"I also like the ledge of snow at Telluride. I can't believe you stood below that."

"With a telephoto lens. What draws you to it?"

"The contrast of the mountain peak and snow, the sky and sun. You caught something gentle and cruel in the picture."

"I'm glad you noticed. I waited three hours for the right light."

"You must be patient."

"Exceedingly. I've been known to wait years, if necessary. Ask Alex." She checked herself before continuing. "This is a departure for me, wildlife and landscape photography. I generally tend to focus on portraits, but this past year, I decided I wanted to try something expansive. I switched to a digital camera. I miss my thirty-five millimeter, but change is good."

I smiled. "Change is hard."

"Impossible!"

"Do you live and work in the studio?"

"Most days, but I have an apartment near Wash Park." She lowered her voice and leaned in toward me. "Tell me something. Leah wouldn't share. Is Alex Madigen as gorgeous as ever?"

"There were no injuries to her face," I said cautiously.

"Leah told me Alex had a head injury. I was afraid—" Clarissa broke off, her forehead creased.

"The skull fracture was in the back of her head."

"Did she have other injuries?"

"Extensive. Spinal injuries, a broken leg, damage to her liver, broken ribs, a collapsed lung. She was in a coma for three weeks."

Clarissa took in a sharp breath. "Did she come close to dying?"

"Several times."

"Will she recover fully? What have the doctors told her? Can she play the piano again?"

"She's making progress every day. She plays occasionally, and she's giving lessons to residents at the rehab center."

"What a relief."

"It's slow."

"I can relate. Once upon a time, in another life, I was in a life-changing accident."

I looked at her candidly. "Were you badly hurt?"

"Irreparably. I'm insanely curious," she said suddenly. "What's your relationship with Alex?"

"Friend of the family," I replied, a rehearsed answer. "How about you? You've known Alex since high school, haven't you?"

"Since the first day of our senior year. It's funny, we met in a photography class."

"When did you lose touch?"

"Before the end of the semester, and it was a bit more intentional than that."

"A falling-out?" I began as a group of five gay men encircled us.

Clarissa hugged the men, releasing each one more slowly than the last, before turning back to me. "If you'll excuse me, Kristin."

"Of course. Good luck with your new venture."

She brushed my cheek with the back of her hand. "Kindly give Alex my best. Let her know that she's never out of my thoughts."

That marked the end of my time with Clarissa Peters.

The men swept her away for a whirlwind tour, complete with fawning stops at each photograph, and I picked my way to the bathroom at the back of the studio. I waited patiently in line until Leah breezed by and told me there was a second toilet upstairs, which she was sure Clarissa wouldn't mind my using.

I didn't need any further urging. I stepped over the rope delineating public quarters from private and trotted upstairs, where snooping soon sidetracked me.

A few feet down the darkened hallway, I ducked into the first room on the left, which appeared to be used for storage. It was filled with lights, stands, tripods, stools and monochromatic screens. Rows of photographs were stacked against one another on the floor, all mounted and framed.

I switched on the overhead light and inspected them quickly.

I saw babies and pets, brides and grooms, and models and athletes, the subjects shot in sharp focus. Some had been printed on canvas and linen in tapestry fashion, while others had been produced in black and white, with pastel accents added.

I was debating whether I should hire Clarissa Peters to photograph me draped over Destiny when I came across the first shot of

Alex Madigen.

High-school-aged, she was seated at a baby grand, turned sideways, her elbow resting on the piano, her hand propping up her head, and she had a faint, self-conscious smile. In the next one, same period, she was standing in a doorway, leaning provocatively against the jamb, staring daringly at the camera. The tails of her white sleeveless shirt were tied up, exposing a flat, toned stomach, and she'd loosened enough top buttons to hint at ample cleavage. In the third from Alex's youth, she was lying on her stomach, chin resting on folded hands. She had long, straight hair, neatly parted, clear skin and full lips, and her eyes were cast down, almost closed. The shot had been tightly cropped to frame her head and shoulders only, but she appeared to be nude.

An interesting development!

I skimmed through at least fifty more photographs of Alex, the pictures evenly divided between the distant and recent past, and among the contemporary shots, two intrigued me. In one, Alex and her dog, Cooper, were seated on a piano bench, the greyhound's commanding pose a masterful contrast to Alex's relaxed and unguarded air. In the other, Alex straddled a kitchen chair, almost melting into its rungs, as she gazed desperately at the camera. I studied it for an inexplicable amount of time, only breaking away at the sound of someone coming up the stairs.

In my rush to turn off the light and avoid detection, I knocked over a row of artwork and gasped at the last vision I saw before the room went dark.

How was that possible? I thought, my heart pounding.

How could Clarissa Peters have taken a photograph of Alex Madigen in a wheelchair?

In a downpour, I drove home from the photography studio, a trip that required all of my concentration to avoid flooded sections of the streets caused by clogged drains. As soon as I arrived safely, I climbed into a tub filled with the hottest water I could endure and soaked until I wrinkled.

After the bath, I went to bed with the Olympus and once again listened to the tape I'd made earlier in the day of Alex Madigen and Leah Stark. This time, I didn't bother with notes. I practically had the exchanges memorized, and several phrases, in particular, stood out again.

Leah's references to not blaming Alex and to maintaining that she and Clarissa would have broken up anyway implied responsibility on Alex's part, but was the attribution real or imagined? To what degree had Alex played a role in their separation? Were Alex and Clarissa sexually involved? Or had Alex merely served as Clarissa's confidante, advising her to break off an ill-advised relationship?

Alex's admission, "We lost everything when we touched," favored the affair conjecture, with "She touched me and I held her breath" adding confirming overtones. But Alex could have been referring to something that happened in high school, years before she met Stacey, years before Clarissa met Leah.

Oh, hell!

This was all so confusing. If only I could reach into Alex Madigen's brain and pick out the strands of memories I needed. Given my frustration after a few weeks on the job, I couldn't imagine the toll the loss had taken on her.

Would we ever know the answers?

I rewound the tape and hit play again.

Thursday, I awoke to full sun, the storm having passed, leaving everything gleaming in the morning light. The change in the weather made me feel downright cheery, a sentiment I sustained until Roxanne Herbert reached me on my cell.

I'd left a message for her the day before, only minutes after Linda had phoned to invite me for drinks. On Roxanne's private voice mail, I hadn't provided any details, but I offered them now, and in seconds, she zoomed from placid to rage-filled. "I can't believe Linda's doing this to me."

"Don't worry. It might be nothing."

"Don't tell me how to feel. Just meet with her."

"Are you sure? I could postpone—"

"I've never been more sure of anything. This lie is only the beginning."

"What lie?"

"We don't own a house in Belcaro. We don't own any other rental properties in Denver," Roxanne said, and with that, she disconnected.

No house in Belcaro? That meant the meeting with Linda Palizzi for drinks did officially qualify as a date. Or maybe not. Maybe Linda had a lead on a property and was just being kind. Maybe she was helping another landlord find renters.

Who was I kidding?

Linda Palizzi would soon make a move and betray Roxanne Herbert—of that, I was certain. All I wanted to do was get it over with, make the tape, file a duplicate for our records and beg Fran to take me out of the decoy portfolio.

Friday at eight, an agonizing thirty-six hours away, could not come soon enough!

I arrived at the office a few minutes after nine, only to discover Fran standing in her underwear, tugging at her pants, the cuffs of which she'd locked in her bottom desk drawer, a scene that had become all too familiar.

She brightened when she saw me, freed the slacks and tossed me two legs. "Here, help me out."

"Why can't you buy these in the right size?" I said reasonably.

"Don't think I didn't. Can I help it if they shrink? Five washings and suddenly I got pedal-pushers. Can't be going to my professional debut tonight in floods. Makes me look short."

"It's a radio show. No one will see you." I held on tight while she pulled with all her might. "And you are short."

"Not that short."

"How much did these cost?"

"Thirty bucks. Target special."

"Take them back."

"Pull harder," she said, grunting. "We're almost done."

I accommodated her with one last tug. "What did you find out?"

"About what?"

"Clarissa Peters. You promised me the report this morning."

"That I did," Fran said, swiftly recovering from the obvious brain blip. "Let me get my notes." She wiggled into her pants, dropped into her chair, licked her index finger and scrolled through a binder on her desk. "Didn't know how far you wanted me to go with this. Started with the legal stuff. Public records, info from pay-per-search databases, so forth."

"That's probably far enough."

"Might not say that when you hear what I found."

I leaned back in my chair. "Start talking."

"Which do you want first—past or present?"

"You choose."

"Present day, C.P. lives in an apartment building near Washington Park, on Pearl Street. Did a drive-by early this morning. Nothing special. Clean, three-story building, all rentals."

"Does Clarissa live alone?"

"Seems to. Been flying solo for a long time, far back as Web spiders can crawl. None of the previous addresses I pulled up overlapped with any other names. Doesn't mean she hasn't had a honey living with her underground, but never shared utilities, loans, club memberships. Nada."

"We'll assume she's single."

"Fair assumption. To continue, she used to work as an anaplastologist. Save you the embarrassment of asking. Whiz who—"

I interrupted. "Reconstructs body parts."

Fran's jaw dropped. "How'd you know? Never seen you filling out the crosswords."

"I ran into Leah at Clarissa's photography show, and she—"

"Leah? Refresh my memory."

"Leah Stark, the woman who came to see Alex yesterday, the one with the healing potions and meditation tapes—"

"Righto! I'm with you. Continue!"

"She told me Clarissa sold her business a month ago."

Fran nodded. "That she did, to a competitor in Minneapolis."

"What did Clarissa used to make? Arms and legs?"

"Think smaller. Eyes, noses, ears, nipples. Only two hundred of these specialists in the country. One-ninety-nine now."

I grimaced. "I can understand why Clarissa switched to nature photography."

"Must be a recent change. Used to do portraits as a lucrative sideline biz."

"How lucrative?"

"Minimum five hundred a sitting, according to her Web site."

"I saw some of those in her studio last night, upstairs in a storage room."

Fran smiled proudly. "You poking around?"

I grinned. "Maybe, a little, on my way to the bathroom. Anyway, there were dozens of shots of Alex, some as a teenager, some as an adult—I'm assuming taken shortly before the accident. There was also at least one shot of her *after* the accident, in a wheelchair."

Fran whistled. "What's up with that?"

I rubbed my forehead. "I don't know. What else did you find out?"

"Lay this on your brain. While our ace pianist enjoyed her freshman year at Juilliard, our friend Clarissa spent time in prison."

My jaw dropped. "Why? What were the charges?"

"That's what I been dying to tell you," Fran said, rising and skipping around the office. "Clarissa was in a car accident the summer after they graduated from high school. Drove her Ford LTD off Lookout Mountain. Crossed three lanes of traffic and a scenic pullout before plummeting off a cliff. Only passenger with her, girl by the name of Cynthia Graybeal, died at the scene."

"No."

"Yep. Clarissa sentenced to a buck and a half. Didn't end there—"

"A buck and a half?"

"Sorry." Fran paused midskip. "Eighteen months of incarceration, but another slice of the sentence continues to this day."

"Probation?"

"You could call it that. At the request of the parents of the deceased, the presiding judge ordered Clarissa Susan Peters to bring flowers to Cynthia Louise Graybeal's grave. She's got to do the deed once a year for the rest of her life, on the anniversary of her friend's death."

"Which is?"

Fran came closer, grabbed the arms of my chair and leaned in. "Prepare yourself."

"Jesus Christ, do you always have to be so dramatic?"

She laughed and whispered, "August sixteenth."

I stared at her, unable to speak.

CHAPTER 16

August sixteenth, the day of Alex Madigen's accident.

I didn't waste any time.

I read every piece of paper in Fran's binder and then left for Sinclair Rehabilitation Center.

At a nurse's direction, I opened the door to the southside stairwell and found Alex. I remained silent as she walked up a half-flight of stairs, paused and, without turning, retraced her steps, descending backward. For support, she grazed the handrail with her right hand.

"There you are," I said, catching her attention when she neared the landing. "You look good."

"I accomplished this a month ago. My ultimate goal is to—"

"Run a marathon?"

She smiled fully. "More like this." She climbed back up the stairs and demonstrated an attempt to come down facing forward. She held on to the rail with both hands and almost lost her balance several times. After completing the exercise, she sat on the bottom step, breathing hard. "Why are you here?"

"Do I need an appointment?" I said mildly.

Alex wiped the back of her hand across her forehead, which was damp with sweat. "I'm sorry. I had a rough night."

"Do you want to talk about it?"

She shook her head. "I'm beat."

"I can come back later."

"No." She grabbed my hand. "Don't leave. After I rest a minute, I'll complete five more sets of repetitions and we can go to my room."

I sat next to her. "I don't mind talking here."

Her chest heaved. "You've come to tell me about Clarissa, haven't you?"

"How did you know?"

"What else could it be? Did you attend the opening of her show? Did you meet her?"

I nodded. "I went, and we chatted for a few minutes."

"What's she like?"

"Intense. She's also very outgoing and personable."

Alex studied her feet. "Did she ask about me?"

"Several times."

Her head snapped up. "You didn't tell her I can't remember, did you? I can't have her knowing what I know."

"What do you know, Alex? Have you seen Clarissa?"

"No."

"Not since your accident?"

Her face went slack. "No. I would remember, wouldn't I? Why do you ask?"

"In a storage room in her studio, I found a collection of photographs she'd taken of you."

"But we know that. She's a photographer. She took my picture for the chorus Web site," Alex said as if reciting.

"She also took pictures of you when you were a teenager and dozens of others more recently. In one, you were in a flower garden, with the sun's rays forming a halo around your head. Does that sound familiar?"

"No."

"It was taken in front of this building."

Alex looked stricken. "That can't be. How is that possible?"

"You were in a wheelchair."

"I never saw her. I never authorized her advances. I would have remembered. No!" she implored.

I put my hand on her knee to quell the shaking. "Calm down."

"Don't tell me this. Why would she take my picture without my knowledge?"

"I have a hunch you two were involved," I said, hesitating as I gauged her reaction.

"In high school or . . . later?"

"Both, and you don't seem surprised. You remember?"

"Parts of my life return in splinters and shards."

"A face-to-face meeting with Clarissa might clear up the confusion."

Her eyes widened. "You're suggesting she come here?"

"Or you could meet at a neutral location."

Alex shivered. "Not alone. I can't be alone with her. Not ever again."

"I'd be with you."

"Did she make this request?"

"No. It's my idea."

"Why?"

"Because the day you hired me, you told me you'd rather know than not know."

"What if I've changed my mind?"

"Obviously, this is disturbing you. Something happened between you and Clarissa, and I suspect it affected you deeply. If you stop now, this could haunt you for the rest of your life."

"You don't have to threaten me," Alex said, tears rushing down her cheeks. "I've been haunted by her for as long as I can remember."

They think I can't remember, but I can.

I was using the crowd in the coffee shop for protection as I leafed through a three-ring binder, thick with letters and notes.

Clarissa brought two cups of tea to the table and sat down. "Thanks for agreeing to meet with me."

She scooted her chair closer to mine, and I rose and moved to the seat across from her. "You said you had something important to discuss?"

"I did. I do. I want to apologize." She paused. "I'm sorry I cried."

"When?"

"The first time. In the bathroom."

"Oh, that." I masked my devastation by taking a sip of tea. "We were young then."

"I know it hurt you."

"We did the best we could."

"I'd never kissed a girl before, but I lied."

"When?"

"When I screamed that I wasn't like you."

"Oh."

"In front of all those other girls. I'm sorry, Alex. It hurt to want you that much and to know that everyone else would hate me if I acted on my feelings."

I closed the binder. "I can't believe you saved all these notes. Even the first one I wrote you in photography, asking if you wanted to do our assignment together."

"I don't know why I cried. I wanted you to kiss me. It's all I'd been thinking about for weeks. I tried to kiss you once, but I lost my nerve."

A long pause followed, and I was unable to make eye contact. "In the darkroom?"

Clarissa laughed lightly. "You knew?"

"I'd hoped."

"Had you ever kissed a girl before?" she asked.

"No."

"When did you again?"

"I can't remember."

"Yes, you can. You remember everything. You used to be able to recall conversations, word-for-word, days later."

"I can't remember."

"I can. Vividly," she said in an odd tone. "A month later, I kissed

Cindy Graybeal."

I was stunned. "The shotput girl?"

Clarissa nodded. "One and the same."

"You always tried to avoid her."

"I know."

"Why did you kiss her?"

"I felt lost when you stopped talking to me and left school."

"I waved to you at graduation," I said lamely.

"I saw you, but I couldn't do anything. Cindy was with me the whole time."

"How long were you two together?"

"Only through the summer."

"Did you . . . ?" I couldn't finish the question.

"What?"

"Were you . . . ?"

"Were we sexual? We tried a few times."

Another silence stretched out, during which I contemplated why this mattered to me, an event that had occurred almost two decades earlier. I took a few shallow breaths. "How was it?"

Clarissa released a sad smile. "Awkward. I kept imagining she was you, but it didn't help. I never could reach orgasm. Cindy tried so hard to make me come, you would have thought she was competing in the decathlon. It was a lot of effort for very little pleasure."

My hand felt imprisoned by hers. I tried to devise a way to discreetly remove it, but it was too late. She'd tightened her grip and begun to stroke my forearm. I stared at the design on the table and flinched when she touched my chin and raised my head.

My eyes met hers at the exact moment she said, "I loved you, you know."

I wrinkled my forehead as tight as my muscles would allow, anything to stop the tears, but one leaked out. "I know."

"You broke my heart."

"Likewise," I replied, more acceptance than accusation.

She moved into the chair next to mine, and the loud scraping drew the attention of other patrons. She hugged me tightly and stroked my hair, murmuring indistinguishable words that nonetheless soothed me.

In time, my trembling subsided.

She used a light tone with her next query, but I could hear the seriousness underneath. "Did you remember the woman you kissed after me? Who was your next conquest?"

Too resigned to lie, I met her gaze. "I never really forgot."

"I knew you didn't," she said triumphantly. "Who was it? Heather in physics class?"

"No."

"Someone you met at Juilliard?"

"No."

"C'mon! I can't stand the suspense."

"I kissed Stacey."

Clarissa's eyes bulged in shock, and she let go of me and laughed long and hard.

I never smiled.

Alex brushed off my awkward attempts to comfort her. She caught her breath, swiped at her cheeks and stood unsteadily. "I can't talk about this anymore. I have to complete my steps."

"What did you just remember?"

She took hold of the railing. "Nothing of importance."

"When you were in high school, was Clarissa your girlfriend?"

"My ears are buzzing, and I have to take my steps."

"After you met again, did you resume your relationship? Did you cheat on Stacey?"

"One step at a time," she said mechanically, not moving her feet. "Don't look forward. Don't look back. Take this step and move on to the next. Fight through pain. Block out negative thoughts."

"Alex, please!"

She unclenched her fists and looked at me. "I would never do that to Stacey."

"Are you certain?"

"I had more willpower, an unbelievable amount of resolve," she said, collapsing against the wall. "With every choice came a loss. When I couldn't bear any more loss, I refused to choose. And in my refusal, I lost everything."

"I'm not sure what you mean," I said softly.

She let out a moaning sound. "I led an honorable life. I did everything I could—"

"I believe you."

"—until the night the planes fell from the sky."

"I don't understand."

Alex's shoulders slumped. "Ask Stacey. She left first."

They think I can't remember, but I can.

I had a date that night.

With Stacey.

We'd promised to set aside time for each other once a week, and this was our first attempt at rekindling. I applied makeup, finished dressing and had just fastened the clasp on the diamond bracelet she'd given me for our last anniversary when my cell phone rang.

I answered it and listened but never said a word. At the end of the conversation, I calmly pressed the button to disconnect and hurled the phone across the room.

I paced furiously in front of the mirror in the bathroom and had to double over to catch my breath. When I straightened up, I viciously washed my face.

At rush hour, two small planes had collided over southeast Denver, and Stacey had been called to duty, the biggest catastrophe of her life. Bodies and propellers had rained on office buildings and houses. Personal effects and engine parts had covered streets, parking lots and yards, wreckage sprayed across six square miles. All passengers on board—three on the Cessna and two on the Piper—were dead, and the death toll on the ground had yet to be calculated.

I glared at the mirror before splitting into a twisted smile, then used the phone in the bedroom to place a call.

CHAPTER 17

Alex Madigen couldn't, or wouldn't, give me any more information in the stairwell.

She claimed the concrete was spinning and she felt like throwing up, which was enough to make me scurry out of Sinclair.

But I wasn't about to give up.

Two people knew the answers to the questions I'd posed.

Alex and Clarissa.

If my client wouldn't give me the responses I sought, I'd obtain them by whatever means necessary. At least that was my justification at the beginning of the stakeout, which I initiated around dinnertime.

Five hours later, however, I was having second thoughts and had begun to contemplate the Global Positioning System Fran Green coveted. Three thousand dollars wasn't that much money, I rationalized. Less than a month's overhead, not including payroll. To earn the funds, we'd have to accept four or five Test-A-Mate decoy cases if I were bait, eight or ten if we split the profits with someone more suited to deception. To save the sum, we'd have to forgo twelve thousand databases searches, at twenty-five cents a click, or two hundred pounds of See's chocolates, at fifteen bucks per. Who was I kidding? Three thousand dollars was a fortune, but was this an acceptable alternative? Was I the only private investigator in Denver foolish enough to be using such an outdated mode to track someone?

My butt was sore, I needed to stretch my legs and I'd adjusted the driver's seat to every position possible, ten times at least. I'd brought three sleeves of Jolly Rancher candies with me and eaten them in the first hour while I studied the owner's manual for my Honda Accord, discovering features I never knew I had. The entire time, I felt conspicuous, as if everyone on Santa Fe Drive were watching me. I'd cracked open an issue of *Vanity Fair*, but every page felt like a chore, and I was about to give up for the night when the front door to the photography studio opened.

Clarissa Peters came out, and I could barely contain my excitement!

My gusto soon evaporated, though, replaced by a pit in my stomach. Unable to do anything but follow at a safe distance, I kept hoping with each turn that I would devise a plan before we arrived at our destination. Unfortunately, I didn't, and when Clarissa turned into the main entrance to Sinclair Rehabilitation Center, I drove on. Pursuit would have been too obvious along the windy main lane. Instead, I found a shortcut and entered via a service drive, sped down the dirt road to a back lot and sandwiched my car between a Dumpster and a twelve-passenger van. Through the van's side windows, I had an unobstructed view of the visitor's lot where, seconds later, Clarissa arrived.

I was determined to intercept her if she headed for the front door or around the side of the building toward Alex's room, but she did neither. She remained in her Volvo, headlamps extinguished.

In order to record the time of our arrival, I tore my glance away from her profile and fixed it on the clock on the console.

Eleven o'clock, on the nose.

Shit!

I put the keys back in the ignition, fumbled in the dark for the knobs to the radio and tuned in to Fran's show.

"Fran Green here, welcoming you to our Thursday night gabfest. Come as you are, stay as you like. Lesbians will be the topic tonight and every night I'm on the air. Thought I'd kick off our tête-à-tête with statistics I've gathered on the average lesbian. Let me share these with you, ladies. Let's see, says here the average lesbian has sex one-point-six times per week and owns three-point-three cats."

I turned up the volume a notch.

"Moving on, she'll have seven sex partners in her lifetime and spend an average of forty-one days of overlap in relationships." Fran hooted. "You know what I'm talking about, girls. Don't pretend you don't. On to other matters. The average lesbian will come out at the age of nineteen—hello, sorority sisters—and is five times as likely as her straight counterpart to have been sexually assaulted or molested. Whoa! No coincidence the av les is two hundred times more likely to be a therapist than a manicurist. Illuminating, ain't it?" She paused amid the sound of crackling. "Full disclosure time. I'm operating a low-budget show, no professional sound effects. For those who missed the visual, which would be all of you, that was me wadding up the list and throwing it in the wastebasket. More truth time. I made up the aforementioned statistics. Every one of them. Why? To show you there's no such thing as average. Call in and talk to me about something out of the ordinary."

"I want to talk about sex," a woman with a husky voice said almost immediately, leading me to believe Fran had had her waiting in the wings.

"Hot topic on a sweltering summer night. Keep it clean. Last I checked, I'm coming at you via public airwaves. Can't be ruffling the FCC on my first night on the job."

"I'll behave myself."

"Go for it. Question or comment?"

"Both. My lover and I haven't had sex in three years."

"How long you been together?"

"Three years."

Fran began to cough. "Excuse me. Mini-moth flew in the back

of my throat." She hacked some more and cleared her throat several times. "Must be a wing left in there. We'll take a commercial break, and I'll be back in a jiff, assuming I'm still alive."

As I stared at Clarissa Peter's shadowy figure, I endured four minutes of commercials before Fran returned.

"Cripes. Sorry about the snafu. Think they'd make these sound booths mothproof, wouldn't you? Heckuva way to kick off the show." She made a noise as if she'd swallowed a large gulp of liquid. "If you're just joining us, glad you could finally make it. I'm Fran Green, and I've got Gemini on the line. The woman, not the sign. Care to share, Gemini?"

I turned down the volume and reflected on why I was following Clarissa Peters in the first place.

The surface answer? Because I didn't know what else to do.

I'd been charged with deciding whether to bring her back into Alex Madigen's life, but I had no clue whether an encounter would help or hinder Alex's recovery. Alex couldn't afford a setback, physical or emotional, this close to her release date, and I felt as if I held her life in my hands, an overwhelming responsibility.

What really had transpired between Alex and Clarissa?

Without a doubt, they'd had an affair.

Had it ended badly? Had it ended at all?

Did the beginning of it, the end or both influence Alex's decision to commit suicide?

My gaze never left Clarissa as I pondered the options, and she never budged.

I couldn't fathom what she gained by sitting in the dark outside the rehab center, but as long as she stayed, I would, too.

I raised the volume on the radio in time to catch a caller's plaintive cry. "Why do straight people stay together? Religion and kids."

"Speaking as an ex-nun who spent thirty years in the convent, I beg to differ on the religion. And plenty of card-carrying dykes I know have kids."

"You're missing my point. Married heteros stay married because they're part of a larger community. What'll keep us together if we're part of nothing?"

"We have a lesbian community in Denver."

"Not a visible one, accessible to all, and nothing in it supports long-term relationships."

"You're hanging out with the wrong women, my friend."

"I have another gripe. Straight people assume me and my partner are sisters. She's skinny, I'm fat. She's short, I'm tall. She has brown eyes, mine are green. I'm fed up that this is all a breeder's mind can absorb. Sisters! They neuter us with their ignorance."

"Tamp down the anger, little lady. It's the power, the way we carry ourselves. That's what they're sniffing out, but they don't know how to express it. Time for another ditty from our sponsors. When we return, I've got a special topic for your amusement. Don't miss it!"

My mind wandered again.

Allegedly, Alex and Clarissa hadn't spent time together since the accident, but the evidence was mounting in favor of a close relationship before the crash.

Alex Madigen became agitated every time Clarissa's name was mentioned. Leah Stark acted strangely around the subject of their relationship. Stacey Wilhite was furious with Alex about something, most likely whatever had caused their breakup the month before Alex's accident. Also, Clarissa Peters had captured at least one shot of Alex post-accident, and in every other photograph she'd taken over the years, the intimacy was glaring.

As I mulled over the facts, I couldn't dismiss the significance of August sixteenth, the day Alex was fired from the chorus, the court-mandated day Clarissa delivered flowers to Cindy Graybeal's grave, the day Alex drove into a concrete column. Coincidence? Not likely, which led me down another path. Who was Cindy Graybeal, and what role had she played in Alex and Clarissa's lives?

The more these threads of information knotted in my mind, the more aggravated I became. What did it all mean, and why the hell was I sitting in my car, watching someone watch someone?

Jittery, I picked up my cell phone and dialed the number Fran had given out to listeners.

After about fifty rings, she answered. "Fran Green here. What can I do you for?"

"It's me."

"Hey, kiddo. How am I doing?"

"You sound great."

"Friendly? Confident? Relaxed?"

"All of the above."

"I'm in a groove, that's a fact. How about you? What're you up to?"

"Not much. I'm—"

At the sound of a beep in the background, Fran said hurriedly, "Hate to cut you off, partner, but gotta go. You'll love this next piece."

"What about my comment on—" I said, only to hear the dial tone.

Fran was back on the air.

"Next topic, commitment ceremonies—what to wear. Choose a dress, and you look like you're in drag. Choose a tux, and you are in drag. It's not all about you, lovebirds. Have the wedding party to consider, too, and Fran Green is happy to help. Bought a book on bridesmaids' dresses at the Tattered Cover. Thought we could turn to our straight sisters for inspiration, but now that I've taken a peek at the tome, can't tell if it's a joke or serious effort. Take these dresses on page three. Looks like they're made out of wallpaper from the Seventies. Page four brings us that material Christo wants to wrap across the Arkansas River."

I smiled, picturing the translucent fabric.

Fran cleared her throat. "Next shot is of some garb that looks like guests threw rice and it stuck to the bridesmaids. Whooee, gust of wind, and these babies on page eight are taking off like hot air balloons. We think we've got it tough sometimes, but it ain't easy being hetero, not if this book's any indication. Am I right or am I right? Call in tonight. Third caller gets the book when I'm done."

I didn't have time to vie for the book, because with a start I realized that Clarissa had started to move.

I turned on the engine and backtracked down the service road. I waited at the intersection of Franklin Street until she'd driven by, fell in behind her and followed her to her apartment on Pearl. I backed into a parking space on the street and watched her enter through the front door. A few minutes later, I saw her turn on the lights in her second-floor unit.

What should I do next? Should I arrange a meeting between Alex and Clarissa?

Yes or no?

What would Fran Green do? *Wing it, baby. Whatever happens, happens. They're big girls. Let 'em go at it.*

That wasn't me.

What would Destiny Greaves do? *Ask for Alex's permission and schedule a meeting. With her input, define an objective, time limit and boundaries. Stick to the agenda and proceed cautiously. Intervene at the first sign of distress.*

That wasn't me, either.

My natural inclination fell somewhere between Fran's gunning and Destiny's diplomacy.

What would Kristin Ashe do?

By the time Clarissa Peters turned off the lights in her apartment an hour later, I'd made my decision.

CHAPTER 18

The next morning, in my sleep-deprived trance, I was ill-equipped to handle Fran Green's robust welcome, a detail that evidently escaped her notice.

"Happy Friday!" She bounced up and down, literally, while I slithered into my seat. "How'd I do on the show?"

"You were brilliant," I said wearily.

Fran did the splits. "Man, did I have fun! You catch it all?"

"Most of it."

"How about that third caller? Was she a babe, or what? I could have listened to her sultry whisper all night. And the weirdo who called in five times, disguising her voice, she was a hoot." Fran stopped her gymnastics floor routine. "What's wrong with you?"

"I slept about two hours."

"Tough break. You sure you want to work today?"

"Positive."

Fran popped up. "Let's get truckin' then. Had a breakthrough on your case."

"My case?"

"The amnesia case. Would it interest you to know that our friends Alex and Clarissa were addicted to the same thing?"

"What?"

"Talking on the phone," Fran said gaily, waving a rubber-banded package of Cingular bills under my nose.

"How much?"

"Every day."

My eyes burned, and my head ached. "How did you get a copy of Clarissa's cell phone bills? I told you not to do anything illegal. No hacking into databases or pretexting."

"Don't flatter me. I ain't that good with research or lies. What you see before your eyes are Alex's bills."

"They are not! Where did you get them?"

"Right there." Fran pointed to the box of Alex's business records, the ones Stacey had given me, which I'd tucked behind the coatrack two weeks earlier. "Bored yesterday afternoon, thought I'd do a little rummaging."

"I went through those files twice. I never saw a cell phone bill."

"Should have looked harder. Stashed under miscellaneous tax info, in an envelope marked sales tax records."

"Damn it. Who put them there, and how did I miss them?"

"Never know, but it's a common mistake. Could happen to anyone. Not Sherlock Green, but anyone else."

"I saw that tax folder and moved it to the bottom of the carton."

"You're slipping, guv. Why would our jingle writer have sales tax records when she sold services, not products?"

"I never thought about that. Let me see the bills."

"Not so fast. My find, my prerogative to relay the information verbally."

"All right," I said dourly. "But I need something to eat." I opened the middle drawer in my desk, extracted a one-pound box of See's Candies and almost fainted when I removed the lid. "What happened to my chocolates?"

Fran adopted an expression of innocence. "Couldn't say. Didn't you buy them like that? Outlet store special?"

"Very funny. Why did you have to bite into all of them?"

She put her hands together and pointed her two index fingers at me. "Here's what happened. Chalk it up to opening-night jitters. Skipped lunch yesterday. Came back to the office starving. Couldn't help myself. Had a hankering for a caramel. Wasn't easy to find in that assortment. Confectioners ought to label their stock. Would save folks a lot of trouble."

I tentatively touched a toffee slab. "Did you bite this?"

"Nope," she said quickly. "Broke it with my fingers. Clean hands, teeth-free. Listen, I owe you one." Fran plucked a Sharpie from her pen can and made an elaborate point of scrawling on a legal-size sheet of paper, talking loudly as she wrote. "I owe Kristin Ashe one pound of chocolates, principal, plus a half-pound in interest. That sound fair?"

I grunted grudgingly.

"I'll take that as a yes. When you want me to pay up?"

I glared at her as I chewed on the two half-servings of toffee.

"In the next twenty minutes be soon enough?" Fran snatched her keys and made a beeline for the door.

"Wait," I said, torn between a craving for sugar and a craving for information. "What about Alex's cell bills? When did she and Clarissa start talking on the phone?"

Fran paused, hand on the doorknob. "Day after the spring concert in March. Went on hot and heavy for a few months, then trailed off in May."

"That's when the relationship ended?"

"Not a chance. Ask me, that's when it began for real."

"What?"

"Work with me, kiddo. You're gaga over someone. You begin the dance by making calls back and forth, day and night, until . . ." She stopped and looked at me expectantly.

I raised my hands in defeat. "You get caught by your partner?"

"Or," Fran said in a singsong only toddlers could appreciate, "you start spending time together."

"Every minute you can steal away," I muttered. "Which means

you don't have to call as much anymore."

"Yepper!" She slapped her forehead. "Finally, you comprehend! Starting to worry about your mental acuity. Help yourself to the phone records while I'm gone. Make for interesting reading. Note the increase in activity last August."

"The month of Alex's accident?"

"One and the same. Page after page of one-minute calls. Stalking, if you ask me."

"Alex was stalking Clarissa?"

"Other way around. Be back in a jiff," Fran said, tugging on the door. "Gotta get you your fix before you get the shakes."

Fran headed east for the See's store on Colorado Boulevard, and I headed north for Sinclair, where I ran into Stacey Wilhite in the visitor parking lot.

"Could I talk to you for a minute?" I said after we coolly acknowledged each other.

"I don't have time. Alex is being released next week, and I have a million things to get ready." She set the laundry basket she'd unloaded from the back of her Chrysler Pacifica on the ground and reached in through a side door to retrieve two pillows. "Alex doesn't like the smell of the detergent they use at Sinclair, and she can't find a comfortable position with the other six pillows I've brought. These are soy nuts," she said, grabbing a Whole Foods bag and dropping it into the basket, along with the pillows. "She has to have them on hand at all times."

I looked at her searchingly. "Why are you doing this?"

"Bringing Alex home?" Stacey snapped. "Because we said we'd love each other, and I'm holding up my end of the bargain."

"Let me help. What can I do?"

"I don't need your help. I didn't appreciate your tone on the phone the last time we spoke."

"I didn't appreciate you sending me to Dianna Wallace without telling me her son had died."

"I didn't appreciate you and Alex—"

"We've been over all this," I cut her off in a conciliatory tone. "Could we put it behind us and start fresh? Please?"

She looked away and didn't answer.

"Could I ask you a few questions?"

"Now?"

"Is there a better time?"

"No. This is as bad as any."

I shielded my eyes from the sun. "Should we move to the pavilion?"

"Ask your questions."

"Alex remembers that you worked a lot and it came between you. Is that a fair assessment?"

"From her perspective."

"And yours?"

"After Alex took her big job as accompanist for the lesbian chorus, she changed, too."

"Did you attend her concerts?"

"I was at the first one. The fall concert."

"How was she?"

Stacey slammed the Pacifica's doors shut. "Possessed. No one else seemed concerned with her extremes, but I was."

"You weren't at the next concert, the following spring?"

Stacey shook her head. "I had to work that night, for which Alex never forgave me. She barely spoke to me the next morning and punished me with her moodiness for weeks after."

I shifted my weight from one leg to another. "You sound resentful."

"I couldn't help it if I found a calling."

"And she didn't?"

"If she did, she abandoned it before we met. I couldn't govern her happiness or hand her another career on a silver platter."

"She's had a pivotal memory of a plane crash. Do you know what she's talking about?"

Stacey let out a derisive sound. "A year ago, in May, three months before her accident, two planes collided in the air over Denver, and Alex resented me for canceling our evening plans. She accused me of choosing work over her."

"Did you?"

"I wouldn't expect you to understand what my job involves."

"I remember the crash from the news."

"Yes, but news accounts couldn't convey what it was like at the scene," she said condescendingly. "It was one of the worst tragedies in Denver's history, and I wasn't the only advocate working overtime. Everyone in my department worked long hours. We had a six-square-mile accident scene to cover. Help was called in from across the state to provide counseling for the hundreds of victims."

"I didn't realize so many people were affected."

"Five died in the planes, twelve were killed on the ground and fourteen hundred homes and businesses were affected directly or indirectly. We set up temporary headquarters at a Methodist church on Hampden, and I was chosen to lead the team of crisis counselors. During all of this, Alex expected me to drop everything to pay attention to her, but you know what I chose to do instead?"

"No."

"I chose to ignore her so that I could listen to victims as they recounted the terror of the night. In the days following the tragedy, I arranged funerals and called insurance companies. I phoned friends and loved ones. I steered injured parties through the health care system and filled out applications for state funds. I held the hands of family members, prayed with them and kept them company. Whatever anyone needed, I provided as best I could. If that meant I lost my partner, so be it."

"You correlate the two?"

"How can I not? The planes crashed in May, and by July, Alex and I had separated. In August, she went on her joyride."

"Do you think Alex tried to kill herself?"

"How do you expect me to answer that if no one else can?"

"What was she like the day of the accident?"

Stacey crossed her arms. "I can't say."

"Can't or won't?"

"I didn't see her that day."

"What about in the weeks leading up to the crash?"

"I'm the wrong person to ask. We barely spoke."

"Why are you so flip about this?" I said heatedly. "How can you have compassion for people you've just met and none for your partner?"

"Alex has never needed my empathy, least of all now. Her life today is better than it was a year ago."

I shot Stacey a look. "You can't mean that."

"Can't I? She has activities and opportunities for socialization. Volunteers fawn over her, nurses praise her and residents adore her. She's the belle of the ball, performing recitals every day, giving lessons to anyone who asks. A dozen people are on her team, concerned with her well-being, rooting for her every step of the way. Everyone strives to figure out what will bring Alex the greatest comfort, but she's not the only one suffering," Stacey said, a catch in her voice. "Where's my team?"

"Alex hates being dependent on people." I strained to control my temper. "You can see the frustration everytime she has to ask for assistance. The people who surround her are healthcare workers paid to do a job. The opportunities for socialization come almost exclusively from other brain-injured residents, most of whom function at low levels. At the recitals, she plays requests, and I haven't heard anything except 'Ninety-Nine Bottles of Beer' and 'Old McDonald Had a Farm.'"

Stacey removed her sunglasses, put one hand on her hip and fixed me with a piercing stare. "Yes, but she doesn't have to give one thought to anyone but herself, does she? No one in that building knows who she really is, do they?"

"You act like she's a horrible person."

"There may be biological reasons for her behavior now, but what was her excuse before? Social workers have told me that she might not be mentally or emotionally available to others, but that's nothing new."

"Was Alex having an affair? Is that what you can't forgive?"

"Why don't you ask her?"

"I have. She can't remember."

"Neither can I," she retorted, an obvious lie.

"How did you find out about her and Clarissa Peters?" I said, dropping the name to elicit a reaction.

Stacey remained stone-faced. "Ask Alex who told me about the affair."

My mouth opened in dismay. "Was it Clarissa?"

"After Alex answers that, ask her who was in first position on her cell phone. Have her tell you who arrived at the hospital at the same time as I did and who's tried to gain access every week since."

CHAPTER 19

Who was the first person to show up at the hospital the night of Alex Madigen's accident?

I would have loved to have asked Alex that question, along with a host of others, but I opted to cede the time to Stacey and return later in the day. I drove back to the office, where Fran Green sprang yet another surprise on me.

"This could be the mother lode we been looking for," Fran said, clearly elated. "Specialty for our agency."

I cast a skeptical glance at the tabletop easel she'd placed on my desk. "Traumatic brain injuries? You can't be serious."

"Never more so." She tapped the flow charts with a car antenna. "Don't limit your thinking to motor vehicle accidents. Think playground falls. Barroom brawls." She rubbed her hands together greedily, almost poking her eye out with the pointer. "Domestic violence. Sports injuries. Gunshot wounds. There's no end to this."

I opened the fresh box of candy she'd set in front of me and plucked out a Scotchmallow and Butter Chew. "I don't think—"

"We can do this, boss. One-point-five million people per year get a knock to the skull. One every twenty seconds. *Boom*, one just happened," she said, jumping up and down.

"You are morbid!"

"Hear me out. We got what it takes—compassion and patience. *Apraxia, aphasia, agnosia, anterograde amnesia*—the terms threw me at first, too, but we'll get you up to speed in no time. We could work for plaintiffs or defendants. Big bucks in determining causes, residual impairment, damages."

"We're not qualified—"

"Already thought about that. Here's how we get around it. Hire an assistant with medical training, pass out business cards at—"

"Fran, wait," I practically shouted. "Stop!"

"Why not?" she chortled, flipping to the next page in her presentation with a flourish that almost toppled the easel. "All varieties of traumatic brain injuries to keep us busy. Focal or diffuse. Closed head injury or penetrating head injury. Ranges of severity, from mild concussion to coma to death. Paula has a full caseload working for neurolawyers and the like, sometimes a waiting list."

"Paula would be?"

"Paula Jackson, the investigator I met at last month's association meeting. Ex-nurse, looks like Kathy Bates, fell off her high heels on the way to the bathroom. Any of this ring a bell, or was I talkin' to myself?"

"Mmm," I said, unable to recall the conversation. "Could you let me finish this case before I make a decision on others?"

"Your call, but you want the benefit of Paula's expertise or not?"

"Do I have a choice?"

"Not really. Better write this down. Gets complicated."

With a resigned sigh, I placed an entire Rum Nougat in my mouth and reached for a block of pink Post-its. "All right."

"Gonna need something bigger than that."

"Fran!"

Fran returned to her desk and threw up her hands. "Stubborn, ain't you? Anyway, I told Paula a little about your pianist case."

Alarmed, I stared at her. "You did not!"

"No worries. Broad outline, no names, no breach of confidentiality. After she heard me out, she suggested you approach this the same as you would a defense investigation."

I broke from my doodling. "Meaning what?"

"Trust no one, least of all the victim."

"Alex Madigen?"

"Spot on. Can't trust her at all. Have to compile a sketch of her life from the people around her."

"I am, in part, but she hired me explicitly because she doesn't trust anyone close to her."

"Confabulation."

"What is confab . . . whatever? Did you just make up a word?"

"No, ma'am. Check the dictionary. I'll wait." She bent over, retrieved the two-pound edition she used as a footstool and handed it to me.

I read aloud, "'To chat. To converse informally.'"

"Not those."

"This one? 'To fill in gaps in the memory with fabrications the narrator believes to be true.' That's the one you like?"

"Bingo!"

"You're telling me Alex Madigen's been lying to me?"

"Cool your jets, Astro. Not accusing her of deliberate attempts to deceive. Forget the dictionary. Here's what the neuro experts say about confabulation. Don't you just love that word? *Confabulation. Confabulation.* I could say it every day."

"Get on with it, please."

"Confab." Fran squinted at her notes. "Verbalization about people, places and events with no basis in reality. Subject gives answers or recites experiences without regard for the truth. Appears to fill in breaks in memory with plausible facts. Catch the pattern here?"

"Alex isn't lying?"

"Not intentionally. More like making things up, believing they happened. Let's be generous and call it a memory disorder as a result of the brain injury. Could be conjuring up memories of events that never occurred or actual incidents she's displaced in space or time."

"Space or time?"

"Out of place. Out of order. Take a typical accident victim. Tells you details of a crash, but might not be recollections of her own accident. Tells you it happened in Omaha, but she's never been to Nebraska. Places it fifteen years back, when it occurred two months ago. Tricky part is, victim believes everything she's saying is true. Dangerous to proceed when an investigation's built on confabulation."

I did everything I could to edit hysteria from my tone. "You're telling me I can't believe anything Alex Madigen has told me?"

Fran nodded somberly. "Not a word. Not without independent verification."

I pressed on my temples, hoping to rub out the searing headache that had formed instantaneously. "And I'm supposed to get this verification from people Alex doesn't trust?"

Fran shrugged. "Just telling you what your job is. As an investigator, it's up to you to curtail the confabulation. Yikes, that was a mouthful! Good thing I went heavy on the Listerine this morning."

"How would you—or Paula Jackson, who seems to be leading this investigation—suggest I do that?"

"Make the maestro aware that some memories she's sharing, which she probably believes with conviction and will defend aggressively, are inaccurate. The more she's aware of the confabulation, the less she'll do it."

"*Some* memories," I yelled. "Which ones?"

Fran rubbed her chin. "That, I don't know. Key to success, according to Paula, is to find out who has the best grasp of the injured party's physical, emotional and cognitive condition."

"Before or after the brain injury?"

"Huh. Let me check my scribbles." Fran rifled through her spiral notebook, creating a small breeze with the speed. "Nothing specific addressing this conundrum. Let's go with both. Before and after the accident. Can't tell you how much P.J. stressed you can't rely on the victim. Have to put together the puzzle of a life one piece at a time. Interview partner, parents, employers, friends—"

"What do you think I've been doing?" I said, a deliberate pause between each word.

"Bear with me. Here are Paula's standard questions. How much time did the interviewees spend with Alex prior to the injury and since? When was the last time they saw our client before the accident? How would they describe Alex, the person she was pre-injury and post. And this—this is critical, my friend. Who has the best understanding of Alex's condition? Who would that be?"

"Stacey, I guess."

"After the accident?"

"And before."

"You sure about that?"

"They were partners."

"Assume nothing. Double-check everything. You need the most reliable informant, even if it's the mailman." Fran closed her notebook with a smack. "Need I say it again? Who spent the most time with Alex Madigen before her suicide drive?"

My car practically drove itself back to Sinclair after lunch, the route had become so ingrained.

In the activities room, I came across Alex, seated at the piano with a young woman at her side. She gently guided her student's hands across the keys, and together, they picked out "Jingle Bells."

I observed from the doorway, and when they struck the last note, I advanced, clapping.

Alex looked up and beamed. "You came back. Stacey said she saw you this morning."

"I thought you might want to be alone with her. If this is a bad time now . . ."

"Not at all. We were just finishing up. Jackie has to be at the therapy pool in five minutes, don't you?"

Jackie nodded but didn't speak, and after she shuffled off, Alex and I moved to a nearby table.

Alex pushed aside a newspaper and half-eaten apple. "I have news to share."

"What's up?"

"I'm not going to live with Stacey."

"She backed out of your agreement?"

Alex smiled faintly. "I did. I can't go back to that life."

"What will you do?"

"I want to try living in the condo I own in Cherry Creek. I bought it before the accident, but I've never spent a night there. If I fail, I can move in with my mother, an option I hope to avoid."

"Have you told Stacey?"

"We discussed it this morning."

"How did she react?"

"Relieved."

"How do you feel?"

Alex took a deep breath. "I don't need daily reminders of how we failed each other. I'm looking forward to a new environment."

"Will your release date be the same?"

She nodded. "They couldn't keep me here if they tried. Next Wednesday."

"Congratulations! If I can help with anything, let me know."

"I do have a request," she said, almost shyly. "I can't remember what my condo looks like. Would you be willing to take me there for a visit?"

"Of course!"

"It's empty. I'll need to order furniture and furnishings, but my mother's offered to handle that, and I've agreed to let her."

"Will you need at-home caregivers?"

"Possibly on weekends. I'll take it day by day." Alex leaned forward intently. "I also wanted to tell you something else."

"Okay."

"I considered your suggestion, but I'm not ready."

"For Clarissa to visit?"

"Not yet. I'm not sure we knew each other well enough."

"You did," I said firmly.

"What makes you so certain?"

"The night of your accident, Clarissa arrived at the hospital before Stacey."

Her lips jutted out. "I don't remember that."

"You were in a coma. Stacey sent her away and hasn't allowed her to visit since."

"Has Clarissa tried?"

"Repeatedly."

"Why haven't I seen her? Or have I?"

"Not to my knowledge. Obviously, she was hanging around the grounds at some point, if she took a photograph of you in a wheel-chair. But as far as I know, Stacey's blocked her access."

"Why?"

"You cheated on her, Alex. She's furious with you."

"Clarissa?"

"Stacey."

"Still?"

"Still."

"She doesn't act furious when she comes to see me."

"Trust me, she is."

"Stacey never did trust me," Alex said absently. "I remember that. Lately, I've wondered if that was the result of my behavior or the cause of it."

They think I can't remember, but I can.

Clarissa was sprawled on a deck chair, and I was leaning over the rail, surveying the street below. I was as far away from her as I could get on the tiny balcony.

"Where's Stacey tonight?" she asked.

"Picking up the pieces."

"From that plane crash? Is that why I'm allowed to see you after dark? Hasn't she wondered about our frequent daytime engagements?"

"If she has, she hasn't said anything."

"What have you told her about us?"

"Very little."

"Did she enjoy meeting me at our quaint foursome dinner?"

"No."

Clarissa displayed mock shock. "Why?"

"She thought you touched me too much."

"If only she knew how much I held back," Clarissa said with a laugh. "It's my turn to ask you something."

I turned to look at her. "What?"

"Have you ever thought about me . . . sexually?"

I folded my arms across my chest. "Since high school?"

"Since then."

"I might have."

Clarissa stood and moved toward me. "Recently?"

"Relatively."

"Before we ran into each other at the concert?"

I turned away and clutched the balcony rail tightly with both hands. "Yes."

She embraced me from behind. "How often?"

I remained stiff. "Often. I never stopped loving you. I tried, but I couldn't."

She began to stroke my breasts, but I didn't respond. "I know," she whispered.

"I wanted to forget, but you kept returning in my dreams."

She nuzzled the back of my neck, and I shivered. "Were they good dreams?"

"In most of them," I choked out, "we're making love, but something interrupts us before I can reach orgasm."

Clarissa reached down to stroke between my legs. Instinctively, I pushed my body against hers. "Nothing can stop us now," she said.

"We can't do this."

"Feel how much I want you."

"We can't do this."

She pried one of my hands from the rail and forced it under her skirt. "Please, Alex. Feel me."

I recoiled and shook my head vehemently. "We can't do this."

Clarissa let go and cried in frustration. "We can't not do this."

I turned to exit, but when I saw the agony in her eyes, I couldn't escape.

I kissed her deeply, a movement that swallowed us both.

• • •

I touched Alex on the arm to get her attention. "Do you remember an affair with Clarissa?"

She scooted away from me. "I led a complicated life."

"In the box of work records, I found cell phone bills dating back a few months before your accident. They seem to indicate that you were heavily involved with her."

She looked taken aback. "Why didn't you tell me sooner?"

"I only found them this morning. The first time I went through the paperwork, I missed them."

She shrugged. "What do phone bills matter?"

"They show that you talked to Clarissa quite a bit. Sometimes for hours at a time, which coincides with the period when you began to behave erratically and stopped fulfilling work commitments."

"Maybe I had other priorities," she said aggressively.

"In early August, Clarissa was calling you hundreds of times a day."

"How did she know to come to the hospital? Was she the one who hurt me?"

"No. A social worker called her. She was the first number stored in your cell phone."

Alex began to hiccup. "What am I supposed to do now?"

"Meet with Clarissa."

She covered her mouth self-consciously. "Is that wise?"

I sighed. "I've debated the pros and cons for days, and I always come back to the same point—that you're starting a new life. If I were in this situation, I'd want to get the meeting over with and move on."

Her breathing became more labored. "I can't."

"You asked me to piece together your life. The best way to do that is to talk to whoever spent the most time with you before your injury. There's no doubt that person is Clarissa Peters. Will you agree to see her?"

Alex put her elbows on the table and used her hands to form an awning over her eyes. "I can't *not*."

CHAPTER 20

"God, I hate this case," I blurted out to Fran Green in the middle of the afternoon. I was back at the office, sitting at my desk across from her, and I double-checked the phone to make sure I'd disconnected properly. "Clarissa's agreed to meet with Alex."

Fran nodded approvingly. "Step in the right direction."

"She's coming to Sinclair tomorrow."

"Good move. Clear the air once and for all."

"I'll be curious to see if Alex remembers what happened with Clarissa."

"You kidding?" Fran raised an eyebrow. "No way she can't."

"Why do you say that?"

"The Cingular trail."

"The phone bills prove they had an intense relationship, but that doesn't mean Alex recalls specifics."

Fran let out a snort. "If Amnesia Alex remembers anything, she remembers Captivating Clarissa."

"How can you possibly know what she does and doesn't remember?"

"Been reading up on memory loss while you were out and about," she said, grabbing her spiral notebook. "Wanted to put these gems in a presentation, but given the time constraints, better convey the gist now. Okay with you?"

"Hurry up."

"Emotional memories. Whooee!" She gestured expansively. "Talk about unforgettable. These doodads are tied to the fight-or-flight mechanism. Any memory that forms in the brain when adrenaline is flowing gets cemented in. Good or bad. Some so strong, they become pathological."

"You're categorizing Alex's memories of Clarissa as pathological?"

"Might be," Fran said, nibbling on the end of her pen. "Bear with me. Brain filters out unimportant details and puts the emotionally powerful babies in long-term storage. Anything tied to emotional arousal, that memory'd still be there. Bank on it!"

I exhaled irritably. "Emotional arousal! Where do you come up with this stuff?"

"Medical research. These are high-octane memories, believe it. Everytime our friend Alex repeated the experience in her mind, memory system switched on, took the memory and strengthened it."

"What makes you think Alex had repeated memories of Clarissa?"

Fran threw back her head and almost fell out of the chair. "C'mon, kiddo. First love from high school? Comes back into her life when she's lonely? They get it on hot and heavy? Who wouldn't replay those? Must be strong as titanium by now. What time's your rendezvous tomorrow?"

"Eleven o'clock."

"Need me along as backup? Don't mind working another Saturday."

"No, but wish me luck."

"Gonna take more than luck. Bulletproof vest might come in

handy."

"You're not making me feel any better."

"Can't sugarcoat shit. You be on guard." Fran slapped the notebook shut. "Could get volatile between those two."

Fran left the office around five, and I spent the next two hours waiting to leave for my Friday night date with Linda Palizzi, the decoy target. By seven, I thought someone had fiddled with the clock on the wall—glued its arms to its face—time had passed so slowly.

All the more ironic that I was late for the date.

I pulled onto Gaylord Street fifteen minutes early but didn't bother to get out of my car. Instead, I people-watched to take my mind off the upcoming assignment. The one-block stretch, originally built as a neighborhood shopping enclave in the 1920s, was now home to a variety of colorful shops and restaurants, the district complemented by flower boxes, antique streetlamps and sidewalk cafés.

At 7:58 p.m., Linda Palizzi drove up in a black Mustang, and I watched as she combed her hair, checked her teeth and applied lip gloss, the same motions I'd gone through at the office, minus the gloss. She went into the restaurant, and I spent a few minutes mustering the courage to click on the Olympus recorder and follow. At the entrance to Rollo's, I pushed through a crowd waiting for tables and threaded my way past diners before catching sight of Linda at a two-top in the back.

"Hey, you," she said, standing. She'd dressed for the occasion in low-rise jeans, a white camisole, no bra, and a coral cotton shirt with wide lapels and French cuffs. She promptly removed the outer shirt, a move I would have saved for the bedroom.

"Sorry," I said, flustered. "I couldn't find a parking place."

"I'm glad you're here." Linda hugged me, mashing against my shoulders and hips. I separated first, and we sat next to each other in an L-shaped configuration. Linda smiled, her dimples deepening. "What can I get you?"

"A Coke would be great."

"Nothing stronger?" she said, teasing me with her eyes. She

leaned back and extended her arm across the seat bench.

"No, thanks."

Linda caught the waiter's attention, placed our order and turned to face me fully. She ran a hand through her hair, tossing it for my benefit. "How was your week?"

"Fine. Yours?"

"Crazy as usual."

"You rented the house in Bonnie Brae. That's good."

"I wish you could have moved in there," she said, playing with the cardboard coasters on the table.

"It was too expensive, but the one in Belcaro sounds promising. Do you have a flyer for it?"

"Not yet. The tenants are still in it."

"What's the address?"

"It needs a lot of exterior work. Painting, landscaping, a new roof."

"I can look past defects."

"You'll have to wait until it shines. You deserve the best."

I blushed uneasily under the compliment. "Er, thanks."

"What's new with you?" She brightened. "Have you been busy with rehearsals?"

"Very," I said, switching gears to the fake life I'd made up for myself as a professional musician. I shifted when her leg brushed against mine. "How big did you say the house is?"

"About twelve hundred square feet. Three bedrooms, two baths." Linda put her chin in her hand, cocked her head and peered at me, her eyes twinkling. "I'd love to hear you play sometime."

I cleared my throat. "Any basement?"

"Unfinished. Do you have a concert coming up?"

"Not until fall. How's the yard?"

"Big. I Googled you, you know."

"Oh, really?" I said, my nerves fraying.

"Kris Constance. Nothing came up. It's as if you don't exist," she said, her tone flirtatious.

"Maybe not in cyberspace," I returned lightly. "But here I am."

"There is a Kris Constance in Florida who's written books on midwifery and the safe storage of handguns in the home, but I'm assuming that's not you."

I laughed, way too heartily. "Thankfully, no."

Linda leaned closer to be heard above the din, and I wondered if she'd chosen this place knowing we'd have to virtually cuddle to hold an intelligible conversation.

Rollo's was an imitation of a European pub, with low ceilings, dark wood paneling and green and red hunting prints on the walls. The bar overwhelmed the space, with young couples and singles stacked three deep, and the restaurant area, where we were seated, was sectioned off in alcoves that held three to five tables each, the tables small and close together. I shifted in my seat, unable to get comfortable. There was no room to cross my legs without nicking Linda, and it felt like my underwear was crawling up my pants. I shouldn't have worn a sleeveless shirt. I could feel sweat trickling, with no cloth to absorb it.

Linda continued her goodhearted interrogation. "How about the Kris Constance who placed third in the Boston Marathon last year?"

I smiled thinly. "I wish."

"You're not on the Mile High Orchestra's Web site either."

"The principal horn player's on medical leave," I said, mortified to hear my voice rise an octave. "The orchestra's publicist asked if I minded if she left his name on the Web site. I said that'd be fine until we make the switch permanent. He has an aggressive form of thyroid cancer. They performed a tracheotomy, and he's undergoing radiation and chemotherapy. Assuming he lives, he won't have the breath or facial muscles to perform professionally. It's only a matter of time."

Linda looked at me quizzically. "Ashley Stallworth is a man?"

Damn it! I had to recover quickly. "Probably named by a fan of *Gone With The Wind*."

"Oh, right," she said, again with the disarming smile.

"If I decide to take the house, I'll fill out your credit application, and you'll find out how real I am. That should be enough, I hope."

My tone had held a harder edge than I'd intended, but the tactic worked. "Absolutely, yes," she said, her attention diverted by something over my shoulder.

When our drinks arrived, she consumed half of her Virgin Mary in a single gulp, and I softened at the display of nervousness. "I'll give you a call next time I'm playing a gig you'd enjoy."

"I'm sure I'd love anything you play," she said, her gaze wandering again.

"Not bank openings or weddings."

"Maybe not those," Linda conceded. She pressed her leg against mine.

I shuddered involuntarily. "How long have you owned the house in Belcaro?"

"I'm gay. Would you have a problem with that?"

My heart started beating violently, but my voice held steady. "No. Why would I?"

"I have to get out of here. Will you come with me?"

"Where?"

"Anywhere," she said, rising abruptly. She tossed a twenty on the table and exited.

I had no choice but to follow, and I couldn't match her pace. I didn't catch up until she came to a stop next to her car, and when she climbed in, I joined her, slamming the car door. "What happened in there?"

"Some guy was staring. I didn't like the vibe."

"At you?"

"At you."

"Oh," I said, at a loss for words.

"You *are* incredibly attractive," she said, reaching to brush back a strand of hair that had fallen across my forehead.

I pulled away and said stiffly, "Thanks." My eyebrows began to sweat, my stomach churned and my throat burned. Maybe I was experiencing symptoms of food poisoning, despite having eaten nothing except candy since noon.

Linda gazed at me attentively. "Do you find me attractive?"

I moved restlessly. "I'm not sure what to say."

"I've thought about you a lot since we met, and—"

I interrupted, ever-conscious that in less than twenty-four hours, her life partner, Roxanne Herbert, would be listening to every word. "That might not have been a good idea."

"In most of my fantasies, you were naked."

The sides and top of the car felt as if they had closed in on me, as surely as if the Mustang were in a junkyard crusher. I felt nauseous but knew I had to continue in order to quit. "How did I look?"

"Breathtakingly beautiful."

I felt hot and cold, dry and clammy, exhilarated and dejected. Breathtakingly beautiful? Not that.

I couldn't speak.

In the glow of the streetlight, Linda Palizzi leaned over, touched my cheek and whispered, "May I kiss you?"

CHAPTER 21

"'Loved ones may feel guilt and blame themselves for doing something that contributed to the injury,'" Alex Madigen said robotically the next morning, her face buried in a booklet. "'These feelings are natural and will subside with time.'"

She was seated at the small table in her room, and initially I thought she was reading aloud to herself. Soon, however, I realized that although I'd arrived thirty minutes early for our appointment, I'd come too late.

Clarissa Peters was crouched in the far corner of the room, staring at Alex, framing her. She hesitated a moment before raising the camera to her eye and taking a series of shots.

"Hey, there," I said loudly.

Clarissa crossed the room to shake my hand, and Alex resumed reading. "'Don't dwell on the past. Put your energies in to the present.'"

"Hi, Alex."

She gave me a slight wave but didn't look up. "'Visitors are encouraged to ask the patient how she feels before introducing other topics. Allow the patient to discuss the injury if she desires, but don't force the subject.'"

Clarissa flitted around the room, clicking away. In torn jeans, knee-high boots, decorative Southwestern belt and tight pullover top that exposed her midriff, she looked every bit the part of the hip photographer. Alex, on the other hand, looked like a patient in rehab. She was as disheveled as I'd seen her yet, in a two-piece gray sweatsuit and slippers, hair uncombed, no makeup.

Alex flipped through the pages, and her voice rose. "'Accommodations must be made for those who no longer fit into their own lives. Relationships change. A new sense of identity emerges.'"

I sat next to Alex and patted her on the shoulder, a gesture she ignored. "Don't take my picture," I said to Clarissa.

"One shot, of the two of you."

"No," I all but yelled.

Alex paused in her study of the booklet. "Get a closeup of my scars."

"Tilt your head." Clarissa moved in, focused and said meditatively, "We both have scars now, don't we?"

They think I can't remember, but I can.

I lovingly touched her scars. Across her upper body, they spread like a web, and I caressed them all. "How were you hurt?"

She stiffened. "In a car accident."

I imagined a shower of glass shards and steel slivers cutting in to her, and it made me quiver. "When?"

"A long time ago."

"Can you talk about it?"

"Not yet."

I trusted the silence.

We'd held it so long, I could wait.

She turned over, and I traced the birthmark in the small of her back with my tongue.

• • •

"Who is she?" Alex said to me.

"Clarissa Peters."

"You know who I am, Alex."

"Have we met?" Alex said, again addressing me.

"You had sex with me enough times not to forget," Clarissa broke in.

"How have you been?"

"Never better. And you?" Clarissa retorted.

"Maybe we should slow down," I interjected.

"I've been better," Alex said genially. "I suffered a traumatic brain injury."

"I know."

Alex glanced down seductively. "I was in a deep sleep. My movements had no purpose. I squeezed hands on command. I was confused and agitated. I made no sense. I performed simple tasks. I took care of myself."

"She's describing her progress on the scale of brain injury recovery," I said for Clarissa's sake.

"You haven't heard the best part. I moved from intensive care to acute care to acute inpatient rehabilitation to subacute rehabilitation. Next steps, outpatient therapy, home treatment and community reentry. Final goal, independent living."

After a difficult silence, Clarissa spoke. "My heart broke when I got the call about your accident."

"Everything in me broke. Doctors kept me in a pseudo coma for three weeks to counter the swelling in my brain. My vital signs were unstable, and a respirator took breaths for me."

"I tried to come to your room, but—"

"They lightened the coma and gave me medications to awaken me. My muscles had gone flaccid, and my bones had lost calcium."

Clarissa stood in the corner, motionless. "I was frantic to know how you were."

"I was weaned off oxygen and taught how to walk, talk and swallow without aspirating."

"I tried everything."

"I've undergone aggressive rehabilitation, up to six hours of therapy a day. Physical therapy, occupational therapy, speech therapy, nutritional counseling, psychiatric counseling."

"I needed a glimpse—"

"I've been through every stage of dying."

"I wanted to let you know we could go back to the way things were," Clarissa said in a low, uneven tone.

"I'll never be the same." Alex's eyes returned to the pages. "'Cognitive symptoms include difficulty in initiating and completing tasks, impaired judgment, short attention span and confusion.'"

I lifted the booklet, which she held on to tightly, and saw that it was a guide for families of survivors of traumatic brain injuries.

Alex continued, unabated. "'Behavioral symptoms include feelings of agitation, uselessness, loss of control, mood swings, withdrawal, lack of interest in activities, inability to recognize how behavior is affecting others, impulsiveness, increased anxiety and frustration, restlessness and sexual hyperactivity.'"

"Why are you reading this, Alex?" I said, noticing she'd chosen select symptoms from the lists.

She licked her index finger and used it to turn the page. "'Perceptual symptoms include increased pain sensitivity and loss of time and space.'"

"Are you concerned you still have these symptoms?" I pressed.

"My concern," Alex said blandly, "is that I had every one of these symptoms *before* my accident. Didn't I, Clarissa?" Clarissa snapped the lens cap on her camera but didn't reply. "My symptoms started when you posed me at the chorus concert. They magnified when we went to dinner with Stacey and Leah and touched. You knew I separated from myself that night."

Clarissa shrugged helplessly. "I couldn't sit so close and not touch you."

"I almost died."

"I don't know what I would have done if you had . . ." Clarissa's voice faded, and her eyes welled up.

"Dependency is another form of death, the last one I must

escape."

"I could have helped. I tried to see you, but Stacey wouldn't give permission."

"I asked her to call you once." Alex gave Clarissa a peculiar look. "I remember waking up and asking for you."

"You remember that?" I said, suspicious.

Clarissa's face contorted in pain. "Stacey never called."

"Stacey was by my side. For days that leaked into weeks that bled into months, Stacey held on."

"I'm so sorry. I could have held you. If I'd—"

"In the darkest time in my life, I wanted you near me," Alex said, lowering her voice, "so that I could tell you to leave me alone."

They think I can't remember, but I can.

Clarissa and I were snuggling on the couch, below a large closeup of me that hung on the wall. Bells rang at the church across the street.

"Do you think fate brought us together?" she asked.

My heart skipped a beat. What did she know? "Yes."

"You don't feel we were consciously responsible?"

"No."

"I do."

I sat up and moved away from her. "What? You believe I devised a romantic time and place to cross paths with you, at the chorus concert?"

Clarissa looked sheepish. "Not exactly."

"What then?"

"I followed you."

I felt as if I could faint. My breaths were rapid and uneven, and I struggled to say, "When?"

"Remember I told you about my friend Tamara, the one who came to the fall concert?"

"Yes."

"After the concert, she told me she saw you all the time in Washington Park, walking your dog around the lake."

"You came there?"

"Several times a week. I was about to give up when I saw you one

day."

I rose and paced in front of her. "You were lying in wait for me?"

"You make it sound twisted."

"It is!"

"It wasn't," Clarissa protested. "It was the most exciting thing I'd ever done. You looked gorgeous, as if time had stopped. I hadn't realized how much I missed you until I saw you again. I started crying, and I couldn't approach you."

I couldn't get over the shock. "Instead, you took it upon yourself to arrange the photography ruse at my next concert?"

"It wasn't a ruse. My friend Beth was scheduled to work on the project, but I persuaded her to let me take her place. I hoped I'd bump into you, that we could reconnect naturally. I had no way of knowing they would choose you for the solo shots. However it happened, though, I'm glad it did. Aren't you?"

I leaned in close to her. "All this time, you allowed me to believe we were meant to meet again, when in fact our reunion took place because of some sick form of stalking?"

Her eyes darted back and forth. "I wasn't stalking you." She grabbed my arm. "Why are you so upset?"

I yanked away. "Why didn't you just call me?"

"I thought you'd hang up on me."

"How odd," I said, in a disembodied tone, stunned by this irony.

"Didn't you ever consider looking me up—even once—in the last twenty years?"

"No."

"You can't be that coldhearted. Not once?"

I resumed pacing. "Once, maybe."

Alex slowly emerged from her reverie and coiffed her hair. "How do I look?"

Clarissa, white-faced, wiped her eyes with the tissue I'd handed her. "Gorgeous."

"At least my eyebrows weren't above my forehead, like the man two doors down from me."

"I'm not sure I understand—"

"The rearview mirror sliced his head," Alex said coarsely. "He's had reconstructive surgery, and no one recognizes him."

Clarissa walked across the room and reached for Alex's hand. "I'd recognize you."

Alex pulled away as if she'd been touched by fire. "You missed the beguiling phases. My aggression and swelling, my weight gain and 'moon face,' my love affair with Oxycontin. Theresa, my friend across the hall, has had four surgeries to reconstruct her face. She has five metal plates in her mouth and forty screws. The last thing she remembers is all her teeth lying in her mouth and feeling for her nose. She lost a sixth of her brain to a car accident and five months of her life to a coma."

"What's the last thing you remember?" Clarissa said, retreating.

"Searing pain."

Clarissa began to tear up again. "I'm so sorry."

"For what?"

"That you're like this."

"I don't know what you mean," Alex said with apparent difficulty.

Clarissa's answer was barely audible. "In here, injured and frail."

"What did you expect when you broke my life into pieces?" Alex laughed, a hollow sound. "That my mind and body wouldn't shatter?"

They think I can't remember, but I can.

We lay in bed, Clarissa and I, relaxed and naked. I rested my head on her shoulder, and she stroked my hair.

"I broke up with Leah last night," she said casually.

I bolted to a sitting position, pulling the covers with me. "Why?"

"I've always been faithful."

"But you told me you'd had a hundred lovers."

She smiled. "Never two at the same time."

"What did you tell her?"

"That you and I are in love again."

"*You told her about us?*" I rose, covered myself with my hands and fumbled for my clothes, which were strewn around the room. I hurriedly put on my shirt.

Clarissa propped herself up in bed and looked on in amusement. "*I didn't want her thinking I'd left because of something she'd done.*"

"Oh, my God! Oh, my God! Oh, my God!" I repeated the words as a prayer, a confession, a scream. I dropped to my knees at the foot of the bed and began to sob into my bra.

That got her attention. Without covers or clothes, she lowered herself to the floor and wrapped her body around mine. "*You don't have to tell Stacey.*"

"What if she finds out?"

"*Leah won't say anything.*"

"They talked about signing up for a yoga class."

"*Leah was just being nice. She won't follow through. She doesn't like Stacey.*"

I stiffened and pulled away from Clarissa. "How can you be certain?"

"*Leah told me. After the four of us went to dinner.*"

"Everyone likes Stacey."

"*Not Leah. She thought Stacey was arrogant and possessive.*"

"Leah said this?"

"*And more. They won't be taking yoga classes together.*"

The "*and more*" hung in the air. "Stacey can't find out about us."

"Ever?"

"*Not now, and not from someone else.*"

"You don't think she suspects?"

"*She hasn't paid enough attention to notice anything different.*"

Clarissa caressed a faint rug burn on my right knee. "*She hasn't seen this from our last bout of lovemaking?*"

I pushed away her hand. "No."

Clarissa stroked herself with her index finger and rubbed the wetness on my lips. "*She hasn't smelled me on you?*"

I wiped my mouth, careful to use the edge of the bedsheet, not my sleeve. "I'm discreet."

"*She hasn't noticed your sex life has changed?*"

"It hasn't."

"What?" she said in mock indignation. "You haven't slowed down a bit? You fuck both of us every day?"

I stood and continued to dress. I put on my underpants and one shoe and chose my words carefully. "Stacey and I haven't made love in years"—Clarissa's victorious look lasted only as long as it took me to finish the sentence—"and I fuck you twice a day. Or four times. Or ten times."

Clarissa studied me. "You hadn't had sex in years?"

"Not with Stacey."

"With someone else?"

"No."

"Alone? How often?"

"Enough."

"Since we got together, do you still masturbate?"

I took off my shoe and struggled into my pants. "No," I said, weary. "I don't have the energy or the need." I omitted the most salient fact, that my vagina and nipples had become so raw and swollen, sex often brought more pain than pleasure.

"Good. When you did, who was your favorite fantasy?"

"You know the answer."

Clarissa giggled smugly. "Me. I'm glad I became your reality. Why did you and Stacey stop having sex?"

"I can't answer."

"You won't."

"I can't."

"Do you miss her sexually?"

"No."

"Do you talk about it? About not getting any?"

"I can't talk to you about Stacey."

"Why not?"

"I scarcely have answers myself."

"Are you still attracted to her?"

I didn't respond. I sat on the edge of the bed and put on my socks and shoes.

Clarissa reached up and grabbed at my hands to make me stop.

"Alex!"

"No. I'm not attracted to Stacey."

"Good. Someday, you'll be ready to tell her about us," she said matter-of-factly.

Careless remarks such as this hardened me.

If she knew me at all, she would have known better.

I would never be ready.

"You knew, didn't you?" I said to Alex moments after Clarissa had kissed her on the cheek and left. "You knew the exact details of your love affair with her."

"Yes," she said, the air rushing out of her voice.

"Why didn't you tell me?"

"I refused to accept that the memories belonged to me."

"When did you begin to remember?"

"Gradually, over the past few weeks."

"When did you know for sure?"

"The moment I saw Clarissa," Alex said, dry-eyed and resolute. "There was no escaping her."

They think I can't remember, but I can.

My heart was racing, and no matter how hard I tried, I couldn't catch my breath.

I'd lost all sense of time and place and had stopped wearing a watch. None could have measured this type of time. I glanced at the morning paper to reference the day of the week but had stopped scheduling appointments. I wouldn't have kept them anyway.

My eyes needed examining, my teeth needed cleaning and my hair needed cutting, but I couldn't be bothered. In some other continuum, these mundane tasks, along with life's assorted others, would be addressed.

Right then, though, I had more pressing needs.

Every afternoon and most mornings, I returned to her apartment for sex.

I knew I had to stop, but I couldn't help craving her.

CHAPTER 22

Saturday night, I was unbelievably tired but couldn't sleep, a contradictory condition that had plagued me since childhood.

On this night, I tried all my usual tricks—tensing and relaxing major muscle groups, breathing deeply, flopping from side to side, moving to the couch—none of which brought relief. Finally, around three in the morning, desperate for a change of scenery, I left for Sinclair Rehabilitation Center.

I told myself I was going there to see if Clarissa was outside watching, but that was a lie. I knew I was going to be near Alex, although I couldn't explain why.

I yawned through the ten-minute drive and barely could keep my eyes open as I pulled into the empty visitor lot. Resisting the urge to take a nap, I climbed out of the car, and the crisp night air revived me. I headed toward the front door, where I muttered a string of curses when I discovered it was locked.

Heart pounding, I walked around the side of the building toward

Alex's room and was surprised to find it brightly lit. After glancing in every direction, I crept closer, peeked through the window and let out a long-held breath at the sight of the vacant room.

A moment later, however, panic ensued.

Where was Alex at this hour? On an overnight visit with Stacey or her parents? If so, why hadn't she mentioned it? Did this mean she'd wandered off and left the facility against doctors' advice? Or was she sharing quarters with another resident, possibly the one-legged woman who idolized her?

I stood still, debating what to do, until the hiss of lawn sprinklers forced me to hustle around to the back of the building in search of a dry zone. In my haste to flee, I sprinted past the activities room before pulling up and backtracking, drawn to the haunting lighting and peculiar sound.

From a distance, through floor-to-ceiling windows, I could see Alex at the piano, elegantly attired in an ivory shirt and long, black skirt. Her back was to me, and a beam of light created an eerie shadow on the wall, forming an enlarged silhouette of her hands suspended over the keyboard, paused in flight.

The sound I'd heard, faintly perceptible through the open windows, came not from music but from strangled weeping, and as if responding to a conductor's cue, Alex suddenly bent over the piano and cradled her head in her hands.

I watched as her shoulders heaved, but I couldn't move forward to comfort her or backward to run away.

We both remained locked in position, until Alex eventually straightened, steadied herself and walked out of the room.

Head down, she never looked in my direction, yet I had the uneasy feeling she knew I was there.

If Alex Madigen had sensed my middle-of-the-night presence, she didn't mention it Monday morning when I returned to Sinclair.

Instead, she began our conversation with, "In my previous life, I had trouble starting things and stopping them. My involvement with Clarissa Peters followed that pattern."

We sat across from each other in the gardens, on matching benches, under an overcast sky. "Maybe you'd better start at the beginning."

"If only I knew where it was." Studying her hands, she sighed. "We had big dreams, Clarissa and I. We planned to travel the world and visit a different country each month. I would be a highly regarded pianist, sought after by the finest orchestras and conductors. She would be an award-winning photographer, her work featured in books and magazines. We could see the future, and the vision was blissful."

"Were these dreams recent?"

Alex laughed, a jaded sound. "Sadly, no. Every one of them perished in a bathroom stall at Roosevelt High School."

"What happened?"

She stared at me in a disquieting way. "I kissed Clarissa, and she turned against me. Within hours, everyone in the school knew that I was a dyke and that I'd molested her."

"That must have been difficult."

"It hardly seems remarkable now—typical teenage angst—but at the time, I unraveled. I left school early and spent the spring semester in my bedroom. I had enough credits to graduate, but no friends or self-worth and no desire to achieve anything other than sleep."

"You went to Juilliard in the fall?"

"On schedule, which fulfilled my mother's lifelong ambition. I didn't object to her plans. I needed to get away from Clarissa and the memories, but I never played the same again. At eighteen, I no longer had anything to move toward, only away from. I went through the motions in New York, but I'd lost my reason for music."

"Which was?"

"The expression of my truest self."

They think I can't remember, but I can.

I sat on the couch, folded in a ball, while Clarissa paced angrily in front of me. The walls around us were covered with photographs of me, some recent, others from long ago.

"It's over," she said.

"Not for me."

"Yes, for you. Especially for you."

"No."

"You know it is. When are you going to tell her?"

"Soon," I whispered.

"That's what you said last week and the week before. Do you love me?"

"Yes."

"Do you love Stacey?"

"Yes."

"With the same passion?" Clarissa asked belligerently.

"No, but I can't erase eleven years in two months."

"Do you want to keep sneaking around?"

"No."

"Do you want to keep having sex with me?"

"Yes," I said frantically.

"Do you realize this is degrading?"

"For you, yes."

"For me?" she said, her voice rising. She gestured violently, inches from my face. "For both of us. We should be allowed to feel passion without having it destroy us. We should be permitted to lead an honest life. We should be free to wake up together every day and live openly."

"I'm with you more than I'm with Stacey," I pointed out, bargaining. "More than I'm alone."

"It's not enough. I'm tired of hiding. What did you have in mind when you set this in motion, when you kissed me on the balcony?"

"I didn't have a plan. I tried to recapture something, something we could never have, something I'd always missed."

"Did you find it?"

"Not as I'd imagined."

"Then why do you keep coming back to me?"

"Because I can't stop."

"And to Stacey?"

"Because I started something, and I can't seem to . . . I'm trying to follow my heart, but—"

"How does your precious heart feel now?"

I blinked back tears. "Like it's felt since high school . . . fractured in two . . . like I've never been whole."

Clarissa tilted my chin until our gazes locked. "I mean it, Alex," she said softly. "If you won't tell Stacey, I will."

"She went with me," Alex said offhandedly.

My jaw dropped. "Clarissa? To Juilliard?"

"There and everywhere. I couldn't stop thinking about her, wondering where she was and who she'd become."

"Throughout your relationship with Stacey?"

"Off and on. More intensely as Stacey and I began to disintegrate. When Clarissa came out of the shadows at the chorus concert, I viewed it as the cruelest twist of fate."

"Why?"

"Because months earlier, finally, I'd vowed to move on with my life." Alex paused. "To stop thinking about her. To not . . ."

"We can take a break, if you need to," I said, concerned with her ragged breathing and pallid complexion.

She swallowed hard and shook her head. "Only later did Clarissa confess that our meeting wasn't accidental."

"She'd arranged it?"

"Yes. She'd seen me play at the fall concert and found out from a friend that I walked Cooper in Washington Park, and she began to appear there. Watching me. Wanting me. Don't you find that disturbing?"

"She must have felt the same pull you felt."

Alex shot me a wry look. "I never could keep to a regular schedule with anything, including dog walks. When her method failed to produce results, she substituted for a colleague at the spring concert. Photography gave her the desired cover."

"You sound resentful."

"I take exception to the fact that she couldn't control herself."

"Could you?"

"Yes."

• • •

They think I can't remember, but I can.

I never doubted her.

I simply underestimated her speed.

Clarissa talked to Stacey before I could, and I was left one Friday evening to pick up the pieces.

Stacey sat slumped in a chair in the dining room, weeping, and I moved back and forth behind her. I reached to comfort her, but she pulled away. When she pressed me, I had no reasonable explanation for why I needed a partner and a lover.

Throughout the weekend, we circled back more times than I could count, always with the same result. In our separation, I had never felt such desperation to connect, and in her exhaustion, I sensed the same. She asked questions, but not many. I searched for answers, but not zealously.

She demanded that I stop seeing Clarissa until we separated, and I agreed, a promise I kept for less than six hours. Though I was in no position to, I made a demand as well. I insisted that she tell me what Clarissa had told her about our affair. I wanted the exact details of the confession in searing relief.

These, however, Stacey refused to give up.

"I waited fifty-four days before I made love with Clarissa," Alex said, trembling. "The night Stacey went to the scene of the plane crash."

"That marked the beginning of your physical relationship?"

"Yes. Stacey broke her word, and I broke apart."

"How?"

"We had a date, and she cancelled it. I remember the exact moment of disconnect as I hung up on her and placed the call to Clarissa."

"The moment of no return," I murmured.

She nodded vaguely. "Do you know what it was like to touch her?"

"Mmm," I said, unwilling to venture a guess.

"Anguishing."

"Because of the dishonesty?"

"Because of the yearning. Nothing could compensate for the years I'd spent without her. I longed for what could have been if we hadn't died at seventeen."

"You felt that way, that you'd died in high school?"

"Distinctly. I came back to her only to find a shell of who I'd been. The ensuing despair followed me like death."

"You couldn't recapture any of the joy you'd felt when you were younger?"

Alex laughed ruefully. "Joy played no part. Once the affair began, everything else in my life fell away. Nothing made an impression anymore. Not Stacey or my career or the chorus."

"That was around the time Henny Carmichael fired you from the jingle-writing job?"

She nodded again. "I lost all sense of time and commitments because they held no meaning. Days too late, I would remember an appointment I'd missed. I was acutely aware that my life was spinning out of control, and yet from another perspective, making love four hours or five hours a day felt natural."

"You were in bed that much?" I said, unable to edit shock from my voice.

"Or more. And when I wasn't with her, I was craving our next time together." Alex smiled sadly. "I'd waited years to be with Clarissa, drilling our love deeper into my mind. I couldn't stop returning, searching for a depth that reality could never bring."

They think I can't remember, but I can.

Stacey and I were surrounded by guests.

We stood on either side of a large cake with the inscription "Happy Golden Anniversary." After everyone toasted her parents, we grabbed knives, ready to cut.

We plodded through many days like this that, at first glance, seemed normal. We attended functions as a couple—a shower for one of her coworkers, a birthday party for a mutual friend, the fiftieth celebration for her parents.

Through them all, we were cordial to a fault, and yet, in this deceit, I felt more pain than from all the other lies combined.

"Did Stacey know about you and Clarissa?" I said when Alex opened her eyes.

"She found out sixty-three days after Clarissa and I became involved sexually."

"How?"

Alex wrung her hands. "Clarissa told her."

"With your consent?"

"Technically no." Alex smiled gamely at my grimace. "I warned you that I led a complicated life."

"How did Stacey respond?"

"Calmly and professionally, as you'd expect. There was no shouting or name-calling. We negotiated our separation liked trained mediators, and I went about the task of splitting our life into equal parts. When one divided by two equaled zero, I wasn't prepared for that."

"You're talking about Stacey?"

"Yes. And when one plus one equaled zero, I felt even more adrift."

"You and Clarissa?"

Alex nodded gravely.

They think I can't remember, but I can.

Each day, Stacey went to work, propping up everyone who had fallen over or apart, and I tackled the task of dividing up our lives.

I combed through albums, sorting the photographs into piles, equal sets for each of our eleven years. I packed boxes. I rearranged our clothes back in their respective drawers and closets, no more mixing and matching, trading or borrowing. I ordered new dishes and luggage and burned duplicate CDs. I cleaned out the desk and threw away stacks of birthday, anniversary and Valentine's Day cards.

I compiled a list of all of our shared assets and devised a formula for selecting and splitting them. I opened new checking accounts and closed old savings accounts. I interviewed real estate agents and chose one to sell our house. I requested copies of our credit reports and calculated what type of condo each of us could afford on our own. I canceled the contractor who had been scheduled to remodel our basement.

In no time at all, I made great strides in erasing the fabric of our lives, and yet, with every step forward, I fell further behind.

CHAPTER 23

On my trek from Sinclair to the office, my cell phone rang, a call from Fran.

Before I could brag about the progress I'd made with Alex Madigen, Fran set off on her own path. "Only got a minute to talk, fixin' to leave for my chamber meeting, but called to find out what happened with Linda Palizzi."

"What do you mean?"

"Roxanne Herbert called me a minute ago, screaming and crying, threatening a lawsuit. What went down on Friday, Kris?"

"Nothing. Something. I don't know." I shook my head in disgust and added snidely, "Roxanne must have picked up the tape this time."

"An hour ago. Give it to me straight. You cross a line?"

"I did my job. Why? What did Roxanne say?"

"Said you tried to tank her future with Linda—"

"Me!" I shrieked. "What did you say to her?"

"Not much. Mostly listened while I played Tetris. Roxanne-baby can't understand why Linda would go after you when you're not more attractive than she is."

"I never said I was!"

"Didn't, but you are. Roxanne moved on to point out that you're not thinner than she is."

"That's not true," I said hotly.

"'Course it's not, kiddo, but have to understand where the client's coming from."

"I did. I do. But why is she turning on me when I brought her the result she expected?"

"Not protesting the result, more the method."

"What method? I followed protocol, every single thing you told me to do."

"Roxie's over there believing you fell in love with her Linda."

"I didn't!"

"Accusing you of trying to steal her woman."

I lowered my voice to a menacing level. "Listen to the tape."

"On my list of things to do, but wanted to hear your side first," Fran said equably. "Rox was especially hot under the collar about the instructions you imparted."

"We had a two-minute phone call on Saturday," I shouted. "I told her the second tape was ready. When she asked what was on it, I told her that Linda had betrayed her."

"That's it?"

"I reminded her not to tell Linda that she'd hired a decoy and not to use specific lines or examples from the tape as ammunition. You told me to do that," I said, my voice fading with exasperation.

In our training, Fran had cited a fatal precedent as reason for the admonishment. A husband in Cleveland, exposed by a decoy service, had shot his wife and the decoy after his wife played the tape for him.

I'd followed Fran's advice. That was all I'd done.

Or was it?

Had I been adamant with Roxanne about not revealing my deception for her protection or because I wanted her partner to keep fantasizing about me? Was it wrong to want someone to remember my "breathtaking beauty," not the ugly lies?

I couldn't answer without lying again.

Fran spoke up. "Might be a happy ending. Linda agreed to go to counseling. Might have done some good for this couple."

"Good for them. Good for me."

After a heavy silence, Fran said, "Sure you don't want to tell me anything else?"

"It's all on the tape," I said lethargically. "Listen to the tape."

That goddamn tape!

All the way back to the office, I fixated on my conversation with Fran, up until the moment I parked in front of our door.

I would never work another decoy case, never, so long as I lived. Fran could offer me five million dollars for an hour's work, and I'd turn it down. Ten million, and I'd laugh in her face. Why did I go along with every ill-advised scheme she invented? Didn't I believe in myself enough to—

My thoughts broke off abruptly at the sound of a sharp tap, and I looked up to see Clarissa Peters glaring at me. Before I could roll down the window, she said, "You set me up."

I stepped out of the car and replied coolly, "Could we talk about this in my office?"

"What's the matter with here?"

Calling out, "How did you find me?" I started walking, compelling her to tag along.

"I followed you from Sinclair. You're more than a family friend."

"True," I said, turning the key in the lock, thankful Fran had left for her chamber meeting.

"You're Alex's girlfriend!"

"I'm a private investigator. This is my office." I turned on the lights and gestured for her to take a seat on the couch. "Alex hired me to help reconstruct her life."

"Oh," Clarissa said warily. "Her life before or after the accident?"

"Before." I sat behind my desk. "Her brain injury caused significant memory loss."

She lowered herself to the edge of the couch. "What *does* Alex remember?"

"I can't go in to details."

"Does she remember the good times we had in high school, until our sexual awakenings ruined them?"

"She hasn't said—"

"Does she remember the price we paid for our first kiss?" Clarissa said, scooting back on the couch.

"I can't—"

"Does she know that I fell in love with her again when I saw her by chance at the fall concert? That when she played, I felt as if she were playing only for me, expressing something we'd never had the chance to express? Does she recall that I arranged to bump into her at the next concert, because I had to see her but was afraid of how she'd react?"

"Her memories come and go," I said noncommittally. "What about yours? Did the reunion live up to your expectations?"

"It did." Clarissa looked away, apparently lost in thought. "Alex had matured into this gorgeous woman, unaware of her own magic. I found the combination of strength and vulnerability magnetic. I couldn't stop touching her as I posed her. I'd drop back to take a shot and return to touch her again."

"On that night, did she know you were attracted to her?"

Clarissa tucked both legs beneath her. "She couldn't have not known."

"You knew about her relationship with Stacey, I assume."

"I didn't care. I knew they couldn't have shared what Alex and I shared."

"Who initiated the affair?"

"We grew into it slowly, over the course of two months, but we knew it was destined."

I folded my arms across my chest. "When did the relationship become sexual?"

"The night Stacey worked the plane crash. Alex stayed with me at my apartment."

"Your relationship continued through the summer?"

"Yes. We were together almost every day. Nothing was more important. We were consumed by each other. Most of the time, we never left my apartment. We couldn't stop touching each other long enough to accomplish much. I'd never experienced anything like it."

"How did Stacey find out about the affair?"

"I told her. Alex wouldn't, and we deserved the chance for a full life, out in the open, like normal people."

"What was Stacey's reaction?"

"She didn't believe me until I told her what Alex tasted like, where every mark on her body was, how she held her breath before orgasm," Clarissa said, eyes flickering.

I kept my tone even. "Did Alex know you intended to talk to Stacey?"

"Yes, but afterward, she fell apart. We fought incessantly, and she stopped returning my calls. I assumed she needed space, but I believed we were meant to be together. I held on to that belief while I waited for her."

"Do you still feel that way?"

"I don't dare feel anything," Clarissa said cautiously. "You witnessed how Alex treated me."

"You won't try to resume the relationship?"

"Why would I? I'm with someone, and even if I weren't, Alex isn't the same, and neither am I. What chance would we have after everything that's happened?"

"You don't love her anymore?" I said, leery.

"I don't know her anymore. Whatever happened to her brain seems to have wiped us away."

"Not completely."

Clarissa pulled at the corner of her eye. "What has she told you about us?"

"She's asked me not to say."

"And what Alex wants, Alex gets?"

I raised both eyebrows. "I think the situation has gone beyond that. You saw her. She'll be coping with disabilities for the rest of her life. The most she can hope for is an incomplete version of who she was."

"Can't we all? I dealt with something similar twenty years ago."

"After your car accident?"

She nodded. "Alex told you about it?"

"Mmm," I lied.

"Then you know that the car I was driving plunged a hundred feet off the highway, killing Cindy Graybeal, my girlfriend. People have told me the car's still there in a deep ravine, but I've never gone back."

"You crashed on Lookout Mountain?" I verified.

"Off a cliff so steep rescuers had to rappel down to recover Cindy's body. My life sentence began that night."

"Life sentence?"

"I spent two days in the hospital and eighteen months in prison, but it didn't end there. The judge ordered me to bring flowers to Cindy's grave every year, on the anniversary of her death. He made sure that a reminder of my mistake is never further away than three hundred and sixty-four days."

"You've complied with the court order?"

Clarissa let out an unhinged laugh. "I have no choice, but no one can control how I deliver my tribute. Some years, I throw the flowers at her and leave. Other times, I sit on her grave for hours, asking for forgiveness, talking to her about my life. I didn't know her very well when she died, but I feel like I do now."

"Did Alex know you and Cindy had been in an accident?"

"Not at the time."

"You talked about it later, sometime after you met again?"

She stared at me, hesitating. "Yes."

"When?"

"The afternoon of Alex's accident, I took her to Cindy's grave."

"Why?"

"I needed her to understand what I'd given up for her," Clarissa said, showing no remorse.

CHAPTER 24

"With what I've been through," Alex said the next day, between uneven breaths, "you'd think I'd be immune to shame."

"Don't be embarrassed. It could have happened to anyone. The shine's nice, but these hardwood floors are treacherous. Carpet runners might help."

Alex was hunched over next to me in the center of the living room of her Cherry Creek condominium. We'd completed a tour of the one-bedroom unit, located on the top floor of a three-story building at Second and Detroit. I'd already admired the dramatic look of the modern exterior, with staggered angles of steel and wood, and continued complimenting inside features such as granite tile, marble countertops, hand-troweled walls and cherry wood floors. I'd been raving about the natural light coming in through the massive windows when Alex had stumbled and fallen.

She gave me a strained smile. "You're too sweet. You know I struggle with balance." She kicked off her slides, rolled up her pants and clutched her leg.

I leaned closer, removed her hand and peered at her knee. "There's a little bump. You might want the nurse to take a look at it when we get back." Alex crumpled and started to cry, strangled gulps. I looked around the room helplessly. "Are you feeling lightheaded?"

"No." She sniffled.

"Does something else hurt? Your chest? Your back?"

"I'm not hurt."

"Then why are you crying?"

"Because I remembered something horrible."

They think I can't remember, but I can.

Clarissa and I stepped out of her car and threaded our way between graves. She led, carrying a bouquet of yellow roses, and I followed five paces behind.

I felt irritable. "You said you needed to run an errand."

"I do," she said as she tossed the flowers underhanded at a grave marker fifteen feet away.

"Why are we here, Clarissa?"

"I told you I had to drop off something." She walked toward the flowers and kicked them closer to the gravestone.

I read the inscription. Cindy Graybeal, March 10, 1970—August 16, 1988.

I gasped. "Cindy Graybeal died?"

"The summer after high school. Didn't you know? Everyone knew."

I knelt in front of the grave marker and propped the flowers against it, straightening them with care. "No. How?"

"In a car accident."

I looked up at her. "The same one that injured you?"

"That would be the one."

"What happened?"

"I drove us to the top of Lookout Mountain, a romantic excursion to see the lights of the city."

"I don't want to hear this."

Clarissa bent to pick up a rose. She straightened up and pulled a petal from it. "On the way down the mountain, we started arguing. She accused me of being in love with you, of never letting go. She said I'd settled for her only to make you jealous. She told me I could never have you."

I rubbed my eyes. "How did the accident happen? Who was driving?"

"I was. I told the police that Cindy pulled the steering wheel as a prank."

I felt vomit rising. "But she didn't?"

"No. I swerved to frighten her."

"Which caused you to go over the edge?"

"A hundred feet," she said with no emotion. "Cindy was thrown from the car."

"Were you hurt?"

"I was wearing a seatbelt. My only injuries were sprains and cuts. I went straight from the hospital to jail and then to prison," Clarissa said flippantly. "My parents didn't feel like posting bail. They called that 'supporting my lifestyle.'"

I rose and took a step toward her. "You went to prison?"

"Eighteen months for careless driving resulting in death." She picked up another rose and twisted the stem.

I was at a loss. "You spent a year and a half in prison?"

"Plus this. Cindy's father convinced the judge to give me a life sentence. Once a year, on the anniversary of her death, I'm court-ordered to bring flowers to her grave. I thought you might like to accompany me this year."

I took a step backward. "You've done this every year since high school?"

"More or less." She gathered the rest of the roses and began to yank off their heads. "I tried to skip once, but Cindy's father called the judge, who sent me a certified letter."

"Did you—" I broke off, unable to continue.

"On some level, yes."

"You didn't."

"Yes, Alex, I did. I hurt her on purpose."

"Why?" I cried in disbelief.

Clarissa hurled the demolished flowers onto the grave and said quietly, "Because she was right about us."

"What did you remember?" I repeated.

"Something had to stop us, but I never believed it would be anything so permanent," Alex said limply. "Or costly."

I held her hand, and our eyes met. "I'm sorry."

"They think I can't remember, but I can."

"You remember everything, don't you?"

She nodded, pulled away from me and wiped her nose with her sleeve. "I never really forgot."

"I was afraid of that."

She lowered her head. "I have something to tell you."

After an awkward pause, I said, "Go on."

"I was obsessed with Clarissa."

"I assumed that."

"I followed her. Not once or twice. Many, many times," Alex said, drawing a long breath. "Day and night, waiting hours for momentary glimpses."

I tried to control my tone. "Okay."

"From October through January, I sat outside her business or apartment every hour I could spare."

"Doing what?"

"Watching her. Wanting her. I couldn't remove her from my mind, no matter how hard I tried."

"Did you arrange the meeting at the spring concert?"

"No!" Alex's head shot up, and her eyes widened into a wild stare. "I'd pulled myself back from the edge. I'd forced myself to stop."

"Are you telling me the truth?"

"I swear to you," she answered urgently. "When Clarissa came up to me, with that camera around her neck, I felt as if something heavy had fallen on me."

"She never knew you'd been watching her?"

"I don't think so."

"Are you still obsessed with Clarissa?"

Alex stood and paced, displaying only a slight limp. "No."

I gazed up at her. "Are you sure?"

"No."

They think I can't remember, but I can.

I started running across the lawn, stumbling around headstones and over graves. I could scarcely see through my sobs as I knocked down pinwheels and mashed bouquets.

On the windy, narrow cemetery roads, Clarissa followed me in her car, circling to cut me off and bring me back. In avoiding her, I nearly tumbled into a freshly dug grave.

I was running, running, running . . . running for my life . . . past the sun scorching the sky and the birds screeching in agony. I hid behind a mausoleum and watched as she stopped the car, stepped out and scanned the horizon.

I knew she could see me huddled and shaking, but she didn't move toward me.

She'd held on to a single rose petal, and this she let flutter to the ground before she climbed back into the car and drove away.

In a shaft of sunlight, Alex lowered herself to the floor in the corner of the living room. "The morning of my accident, I remember carrying these boxes and placing them here. They contain everything I own."

"That's it?" I said, surveying the ten or twelve stacked cartons.

"That's it. Little in my previous life meant anything to me."

"What else did you do on August sixteenth? Did you see Clarissa?"

"Yes. She took me to Mount Olivet and showed me a grave."

"Cindy Graybeal's?"

"You knew?"

"The accident turned up in a background check on Clarissa."

Alex rocked back and forth. "It wasn't an accident. Did you know that?"

"No. Nothing indicated otherwise. How do you know it was

intentional?"

"Clarissa told me as she threw flowers on Cindy's grave."

"Her court-ordered duty," I said, nodding. "Why did she confess?"

"To hurt me. To prove the price she'd paid for our love."

"Who was Cindy Graybeal?"

"Someone Clarissa turned to after I left Roosevelt High early."

"A girlfriend?"

"A substitute," Alex said in a hushed tone.

"What happened that day at the cemetery?"

"After she told me about Cindy, I ran. I had to get as far away from her as I could, as if my life depended on it. She followed me in her car for a while but eventually left. I walked home."

I stared at her in amazement. "You walked from Mount Olivet to central Denver. That's at least fifteen miles."

She shrugged. "I lost track of time. I didn't forget about the dress rehearsal. It simply didn't mean anything to me. Nothing did. I had to put an end to it."

"Your life?"

"Yes," she whispered.

"You don't know that," I said, my voice strained. "No one does for sure. Accident reconstruction experts aren't even certain what happened that night."

"I am."

"You could have become distracted, reached into the backseat for something."

"No."

"Switched radio stations."

She looked at me with pity. "No."

"Fallen asleep."

"No."

"A driver could have cut you off," I said, stricken. "That happens all the time."

"No, Kris. I told you, I remember everything."

• • •

They think I can't remember, but I can.

In a daze, I staggered down a busy commercial street.

I was disheveled and confused, and I kept shaking my hands repeatedly as I tried to make my way back home.

Except that I had no home.

I walked down a quiet residential street and paused to bend over, unable to catch my breath. After a few minutes, I resumed my journey but soon had to halt, doubled over again. I was consumed by grief but didn't know what to do or where to turn.

That's when I decided to go for a drive.

"I couldn't go fast enough," Alex said languidly.

"The night of your accident?"

She dipped her head in affirmation. "Suddenly, I lost control of the vehicle and panicked. I didn't know what else to do, except shut my eyes and let go."

Goose bumps formed on my arms. "You took your hands off the steering wheel?"

"I'd held on for so long, I needed a release."

"What happened next?"

"The car flipped in the air, and I felt the sensation of flying."

"You left the car?"

"It was the most fabulous feeling, this glorious flight. Until I landed."

"Mmm." I groaned involuntarily.

"In those split seconds in the air, when gravity had released me from the earth, I felt uninhibited," she said from a dreamlike state. "For the first time in my life, I was completely free."

"Do you remember anything else?"

"I hit the ground and became numb and had trouble breathing. I lay still in surrender, ready to die."

"You were still conscious?"

"I must have been, because I was aware of strangers touching me, and I was soothed by how much they cared. Soon, I flew again."

"In the medical helicopter?"

"Yes." She shook her head violently and met my gaze. "Do you believe in redemption?"

"Absolutely. Hourly and lifetime."

"The day we met, you mentioned how hard I'd worked to regain my health. Do you remember that?"

"Vividly. You replied that you wanted your independence back."

"It was more than that," Alex said, unblinking. "Crawling away from death, that was my redemption."

CHAPTER 25

I felt an incredible sense of sadness after I took Alex Madigen back to Sinclair.

In less than a year, she'd gone from moving boxes into her condo in Cherry Creek to staying in the intensive care unit of a hospital to living in a rehabilitation facility and now back to the condo to try again for a healthier life.

My mood didn't shift until Fran Green got her hands on me back at the office. As soon as I stepped through the door, she sprang from behind her desk and suffocated me in a hug.

After releasing me, she stepped back, cocked her head and looked at me playfully. "You're the shy one, ain't you?"

"What's the context?" I said, wary.

"Listened to the tape you made of Linda Palizzi."

I began to sweat. "And?"

"Told you not to throw yourself at the target, but wasn't expecting the teen virgin act."

"I did the best I could," I said defensively.

"Sure you did."

Fran dropped into her chair, and I followed suit in mine. "I hated it. Could you tell that from the tape?"

"Put it this way," she said, sucking her teeth. "Hope our independent contractors have a tad more flow. Reckon gals either got it, or they don't."

"I don't. I tried to tell you that all along."

"Should have had you practice on men first. Not too late."

"Forget it!"

"You shed a tear when the target called you beautiful, didn't you?"

I could feel myself blushing. "Was it that obvious?"

"Only to a pro like myself. Doubt the client caught on."

"I know the breakdown wasn't professional, but I couldn't control it. She took me by surprise."

Fran rolled her chair next to mine and patted me on the knee. "Go easy on yourself. First decoy case. Next time—"

"Would you listen to me?" I cried, pushing her away. "That was my first and last. No more!"

She shrugged indifferently. "Why didn't you say so? Not everyone's cut out for the domestics. Half the investigators I know won't touch 'em."

"Now you tell me."

"Best you save your emotional energy for a real relationship. Speaking of, what time you picking up Destiny?"

"Four o'clock."

"What you got planned for tonight?"

"Twelve hours of sex," I said facetiously.

"Sounds good." Fran grinned. "What time you want me there?"

I couldn't conceal a smile. "Very funny."

Destiny and I didn't last twelve hours, but we did post a respectable showing.

I stretched muscles I never knew I had and could barely make it out of bed the next morning, but after a long, hot shower and lingering goodbye, I smiled all the way to Sinclair.

Pulling up to the rehabilitation center, I saw a van idling in front of the entrance, with Alex Madigen standing behind it, surrounded by staff members. She looked radiant, in a silk-wrap dress and jade drop earrings, and in the middle of hugging the dietician, she spotted me and lit up. "I was afraid you weren't coming," she said, motioning for me to approach.

"I wouldn't have missed your big moment."

"My big moment." She laughed, an enchanting sound. "I'm coming back this afternoon for outpatient therapy."

"Still, it's a huge accomplishment."

She embraced me. "I couldn't have done it without you."

"You did all the hard work."

"But you were by my side." Alex took my hands and held them tightly. "I needed that, not to be alone anymore."

I inclined my head toward the nurses and therapists who mingled around us. "I don't think you'll ever be completely alone."

"I hope not. I'm looking forward to the days ahead. I'm not certain what to include in them, but I know what to exclude. No more strained partnership with Stacey. No more regrets about abandoning music. No more jingle writing. No more living in the past at the expense of the present. Most importantly, no more Clarissa Peters."

"Good!" I let go of her grip and backed up a step. "I'm proud of you."

"I'm proud of myself."

"You didn't really need my help remembering, did you?"

"I did," she protested, her eyes clear and sparkling. "Thanks to you, I was able to put the memories in order and fill in the blanks. You helped me reach acceptance and release."

"You deserve happiness," I said with deep feeling.

She smiled faintly. "I understand that now."

We chatted for a few more minutes until it was time for her to leave. She climbed into the van and settled in the middle row of seats, and as the driver disengaged the steps and slid the door shut, she began to cry. The van pulled away, and I waved at her crazily, her last words echoing in my mind.

I'm ready to get back to the person I am.

Case closed, I thought, a self-satisfied sigh escaping.

Time to celebrate with a trip to See's. I'd pick up a bag of chocolate-covered raisins for me, a box of peanut brittle for Fran, maybe a handful of caramels to share . . . the possibilities were endless.

EPILOGUE

A month later, on a rainy July afternoon, I came into the office to find Fran Green hovering over my desk.

"Package came for you," she said, eyeing the parcel as if it were a bomb.

I took off my Windbreaker and hung it on the coatrack. "What is it?"

"No clue. Didn't want to pry."

"Since when?"

Fran smiled. "Didn't have time. You just missed the courier. Return address Alexandra Madigen. Far as I got."

"Hmm," I said, turning over the large envelope in my hands.

"Maybe it's a thank-you gift, acknowledgment of a job well done. Pound of See's, if she knows you at all. Open 'er up and let's dig in!"

I grabbed scissors from my pen can, slashed the wrapping and pulled out a leather-bound book.

"Dang! No chocolate!" Fran slapped her knee. "What you got there?"

"It's a journal," I said thoughtfully.

"Keepsake for your intimate musings?"

I opened to the first page. "For hers. It's full of writing."

Fran's eyes widened. "Read me a paragraph. Hope it's steamy."

"'They think I can't remember, but I can,'" I said slowly, my throat tightening as my voice carried Alex Madigen's words. "'Every weekday afternoon, I vow never to come again. I sense I have reached a point beyond all reason, but I can't stop. Watching her. Wanting her. In the waning light of winter, I stay for hours, often until long past the moment of darkness. I feel helpless to do anything but stare, stare at her silhouette. These are the last images I remember before millions of my brain cells died.'"

"Egad!" Fran shouted.

With a sickening feeling, I flipped to another page and read to myself.

They think I can't remember, but I can. I sat in my car, staring at a three-story, brick building, waiting for the woman who lived in the southeast corner of the second floor to arrive. This wasn't my first vigil, nor my last. At five o'clock, a late-model Volvo pulled up and parked five car lengths ahead of my Toyota.

"More," Fran cried. "Don't leave me in suspense. Gimme the dirt."

Ignoring her outstretched arms, I began to skim through the pages at blazing speed, absorbing only snatches, my heart beating wildly with every word, my eyes watering.

When I came to the last entry, I dropped the journal and ran out of the office as fast as I could.

They think I can lead a normal life, but I can't.

I haven't had a full night's sleep in almost a month, not since I left Sinclair.

Every night, I go to bed at eleven, but on the hour, every hour, I rise. I peer through the slats of my bedroom blinds and see her out there, sitting

in her Volvo.
  Watching me.
  Wanting me.
  She stays for hours, often until long past the moment of light.
  I feel helpless to do anything but stare, stare at her silhouette.

Publications from Spinsters Ink

P.O. Box 242
Midway, Florida 32343
Phone: 800-301-6860
www.spinstersink.com

MERMAID by Michelene Esposito. When May unearths a box in her missing sister's closet she is taken on a journey through her mother's past that leads her not only to Kate but to the choices and compromises, emptiness and fullness, the beauty and jagged pain of love that all women must face.

ISBN 978-1-883523-85-5 $14.95

ASSISTED LIVING by Sheila Ortiz-Taylor. Violet March, an eighty-two-year-old resident of Casa de los Sueños, finally has the opportunity to put years of mystery reading to practical use. One by one her comrades, the Bingos, are dying. Is this natural attrition, or is there a sinister plot afoot? ISBN 978-1-883523-84-2 $14.95

NIGHT DIVING by Michelene Esposito. *Night Diving* is both a young woman's coming-out story and a 30-something coming-of-age journey that proves you can go home again.

ISBN 978-1-883523-52-7 $14.95

FURTHEST FROM THE GATE by Ann Roberts. *Furthest from the Gate* is a humorous chronicle of a woman's coming of age, her complicated relationship with her mother and the responsibilities to family that last a lifetime.   ISBN 978-1-883523-81-7 $14.95

Visit

Spinsters Ink

at

SpinstersInk.com

or call our toll-free number

1-800-301-6860